In the elemental ~~...~~ ... ...g,
but gaining it can get you killed.

OMENS & ARTIFACTS

Setting up shop as an antiquities hunter means nothing if you don't have clients. Benjamin Vecchio, nephew of a famed vampire assassin, is the subject of widespread speculation, but so far that speculation hasn't translated into work.

What Ben needs is a job. A big job. A profitable job.

A *legendary* job.

Finding the lost sword of Brennus the Celt, the mythical Raven King of the British Isles, would make Ben's reputation in the immortal world, but it could also draw dangerous attention. The Raven King's gold hoard isn't famous for being easy to find. Luckily, Ben has his own legend at his side.

Tenzin is a wind vampire who doesn't like digging, but she's more than happy to let Ben do the dirty work while she provides the muscle he needs to make other immortals pay attention. They're partners. Or so Ben thinks.

But when finding this treasure puts Tenzin's future plans at risk, will their partnership survive? Tenzin isn't used to taking orders from anyone, particularly from a young human who used to be her student. Digging into ancient Scottish history can get you dirty. It can also get you killed.

Recd. 7-24-18
from daughter Pam
To Mom Tedali

OMENS & ARTIFACTS

ELIZABETH HUNTER

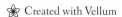

For Lora
Who knew all the spoilers

PROLOGUE

New York City
2016

S HE STARED AT THE BLANK white wall, mentally placing the weapons she would hang there. The bustle of traffic was barely audible on the top floor of the factory on Mercer Street. The building was old but renovated with the highest level of care. Luxury with character, the agent had advertised.

But Tenzin didn't care about the luxury below her. She didn't care about the discreet doorman. She didn't care about the stunning view of the New York City skyline.

The massive loft had twelve-foot ceilings, a roof terrace, and nearly three thousand square feet for sparring. There was another two thousand square feet below them that functioned as office space and sometimes a basketball court for certain humans with insomnia.

Ben had chosen well.

It wasn't as spacious as her warehouse in Southern California, but if Ben insisted on living in New York City, then this would do. When the shutters closed over the giant windows during the day and Tenzin was alone, the loft almost reminded her of one of her favorite mountain caves in Nepal.

Almost.

But she couldn't decide how to organize her swords. Should she line them up in neat rows? Organize them by size? Arrange them in order of usefulness, historical era, or just make it random?

Such a large blank wall. So many choices.

Ben had introduced her to an entire television network that was focused on home and interior design, but there were few shows that spoke to her specific needs. It was rare for Americans to decorate extensively with weapons. And as a wind vampire, the wall needed to look good both from the ground and the air. She'd fixated on the question for weeks now but still wasn't sure what she wanted to do. She couldn't go out in sunlight, but she didn't sleep either.

Tenzin's surroundings had always been important to her. If she was going to spend twelve or more hours a day limited to the indoors, they had to be.

A polite chime echoed from the kitchen on the other end of the loft. Tenzin set down the hammer and nails she'd been holding, picked up a throwing dagger, and walked warily toward the sleek silver machine that sat on the counter.

"This is Cara." The delicate lilt of a woman's Irish accent filled the space. "You have an incoming voice call from Benjamin Vecchio. Shall I accept?"

Tenzin frowned and tried to remember what she was supposed to do. The voice didn't belong to a real person, Ben had told her. It was something called a "virtual assistant." Like a tiny day-person who lived in the computer. Tenzin found the whole concept very odd. If you were going to keep a servant, why not just hire a living one that could also provide blood?

"Shall I accept?" the voice asked again.

It might be a trick. Benjamin was in London and had no reason to call her.

And if he did call her, he'd probably ask what she was doing. Tenzin guessed "pounding nails into your walls so I can hang my knife and sword collection" wouldn't elicit a positive response.

"Shall I accept the call from Benjamin Vecchio?"

"No?"

"Very well," Cara said. "Sending Benjamin Vecchio to voice mail."

The voice went silent and Tenzin relaxed.

The polite Irish woman was hooked into the Nocht voice-recognition system that had been installed in the loft two weeks before. One of the Dublin vampires had flown to New York to oversee its installation and customization. "Cara" could run the computers, security systems, and communications. All without a vampire needing to touch a button. It was voice command. Everything was voice command.

At first Tenzin had been suspicious of the voice that came out of nowhere. It felt like she was never alone. As if she were being watched or monitored by something she couldn't see. The omniscience of the polite voice unnerved her.

But the first time Tenzin had shouted, "All I want to do is watch *Property Brothers!*" into the empty loft and the voice had answered, "This is Cara, and I'd be happy to assist you," Tenzin decided she and Cara could be friends.

Cara chimed again. "Benjamin Vecchio has left you a voice mail. Would you like to listen to it now?"

She narrowed her eyes. "Yes?"

Ben's voice filled the room. "Tenzin, I know you're there. The security monitor in the loft shows me there's someone small flying around the room, so it better be you. Do *not* put holes in my walls. I'm going to call again in five minutes. Tell Cara to accept the call."

Tenzin glanced at the open doors of the roof terrace and considered going out for a short flight just to spite him. She *was* being watched. How annoying. And efficient. Her paranoid nature was forced to admire Ben's cunning.

Cara spoke again. "You have an incoming voice call from Benjamin Vecchio. Shall I accept?"

"That was *not* five minutes." She eyed the terrace doors. Then she eyed the sleek silver box that housed Cara.

"Shall I accept?"

Tenzin flopped down on the Persian rug that covered the floor in front of the media center. "Fine." She tossed the throwing dagger end over end, catching it before it stabbed her face. "Accept call."

"Is Cara working?" Ben asked. "There weren't any hiccups in the system when I left. What took you so long to answer?"

"I was deciding if I wanted to talk to you or not."

He sighed. "Tenzin."

She smiled at the irritation in his sigh. He was so delightfully stuffy sometimes.

"If I'm calling you from London, there's a reason," Ben said. "So the next time I call, can you just answer so we don't have to waste ten minutes?"

"That's not true." She tossed the dagger again, higher

this time. "You called the other day to ask me how my night was and tell me about your research at the library."

"What?"

"I am pointing out that there wasn't any reason for that conversation, so your previous statement was untrue." She caught the flipping blade between her palms. "But I know you are prone to hyperbole, so I won't hold it against you."

"Is Cara working or not?"

Tenzin called out, "Cara, are you working?"

Cara answered, "I can run a systems check if you would like. In order to run a systems check, all current operations will need to be ended. Would you like to end your voice call now?"

Ben started, "No, don't—"

"Yes," Tenzin said. "End call and... run systems check."

Ben's voice cut off mid objection, and Tenzin laughed.

A moment later, Cara spoke up. "I am currently running a systems check. You have an incoming voice call from Benjamin Vecchio. Shall I end systems check and accept call?"

"Sure." She flipped the dagger in the air again, catching it on the way down.

"Dammit, Tenzin, will you cut this out!"

"I think Cara is working correctly," she said. "But she had to cancel the systems check to answer your call. I hope you didn't mess up her programming, Benjamin." She flipped the dagger again. This time it went so high it stuck in the ceiling.

Tenzin winced. Ben wasn't going to like that.

"I'm in London, and I need you to fly over here. Can you just do that? Meet me at that house I rented last summer. I've got a line on something big. Something that could really get our name out there. Other than the Aztec

5

artifact we recovered for that friend of Gio's, the phone has been dead for months. If we pull this job off, I don't think we'll ever worry about finding work again."

Tenzin curled her lip. "But... my weapons just arrived. I was hoping to hang them up before you got back."

"Do not put holes in my walls, Tenzin."

"You told me I could bring my weapons if I moved out here with you."

"You can hang and display *some* of them. Properly. With brackets mounted by an actual contractor. Not random nails pounded into my walls, Tiny. Put the hammer down."

She flew up and grabbed the dagger out of the ceiling, then landed on the Persian rug and brushed away the plaster dust. "I don't have a hammer. I have a knife." She looked up. "And the hole in the ceiling isn't even noticeable from the floor."

"What hole in the ceiling?"

"I suppose I can come to London, but can you have someone hang my stuff up while we're gone?" An idea struck her. "Cara, can you help me with that?"

"What hole, Tenzin? There wasn't a hole in the ceiling when I left."

Cara said, "What can I help you with?"

"Can you find someone to hang up my weapons while I'm in London?"

"What hole are you talking about, Tenzin?"

Cara said, "Let me look." There was a pause. "I can e-mail you a list of general contractors within a five-mile radius. I can also e-mail you a list of custom firearms cabinet builders. Is that what you're looking for?"

Ben was muttering curses. "There better not be any holes in the ceiling. So help me, if there are holes—"

"Send me a list of contractors," Tenzin said. "I don't own any guns."

"Very well."

"Ben, I'll see you in London in a few days." Tenzin tossed the dagger back on the pile. "Cara and I need to find a contractor, then I'll fly over there."

"Do not hire a contractor, Tiny. The loft is not yours, it's mine."

"Technically it's Gio's, isn't it?"

"Technically it belongs to a corporation that doesn't exist, and it doesn't matter because *do not hire a contractor without me!*"

"I'll see you in a couple of days," Tenzin said. "Cara, end call."

"Tenzin—"

"Ending call now," Cara said.

A soothing silence swept into the room along with a gust of wind from the terrace doors.

"Is there anything else I can assist you with, Tenzin?" Cara asked.

She didn't really want to hire a contractor. She wanted to hang the weapons herself. But it was so fun imagining Ben's face turning red, she decided to let him stew until she met with him.

Tenzin walked over to the blank wall again. "Are there any reruns of *Divine Design*?"

"One moment please... There are five episodes currently streaming online. Would you like to watch one?"

Tenzin grinned. "Excellent."

1

London, England

BEN STEPPED OUT OF THE tube station at Ladbroke Grove and turned left, dodging the two laughing mothers in Eritrean scarves pushing strollers up the road. He ducked into the Tesco a block up. He wanted Indian food and beer, but he didn't want to order delivery or go out. He didn't want to talk to anyone. He could barely tolerate the brush of fellow shoppers.

He was in a foul mood.

It was cold and damp. The sun had set at four thirty, and the fog had fallen with the dark. Even more than the damp weather, hunger, and crankiness was the impatience of *waiting*. He'd been in a holding pattern since he'd spoken to Tenzin a week ago. He'd expected her two, maybe three, days after they'd spoken.

So far, nothing. Not a single blessed sign of her, and he was hitting a brick wall with his research.

He didn't have many friends in London. Gavin was in New York at his new bar. He'd called the house in Rome and tried to get Fabi to come visit him, but the sun-loving girl's only response was a laugh. Even Tenzin seemed to be avoiding him. She was probably at home, tucked into their clean and spacious new loft, putting holes in the walls with manic glee while his own boxes sat unopened in a corner of the office.

Yep. Really foul mood.

Ben worked his way through the after-work crowds to grab a tray of lamb korma and a pack of Sharp's pale ale before he headed to the self-checkout. He didn't even want to talk to the clerk at the front of the store.

He'd spoken to every early Celtic collector who would respond to him. He'd interviewed several professors and dug into old land records, but until he could meet with Gemma—and hopefully Tywyll—he was stymied. And until Tenzin got to London, he didn't want to meet with either of those two, because he was more than happy to admit he was out of his depth when it came to teasing information out of very old vampires.

Why was the damn line taking so long? He craned his neck to look around the older woman in front of him.

One machine working. Perfect.

He'd met Terrance Ramsay for a drink the night after he'd landed at Heathrow. The vampire in charge of London was an old family friend of his uncle's. The VIC was also neck deep in dealing with massive vampire political shifts in the Mediterranean at the moment and didn't have much time to worry about lost treasures that no one born after 1000 AD really thought existed.

His tired gaze landed on two teenagers who ambled in, suspiciously close to a woman with a diaper bag and a stroller. Ben narrowed his eyes as they moved closer.

Dammit, he was going to have to talk to someone or

they'd have her wallet in seconds.

Just then, the woman's toddler let out a high-pitched shriek and the boys changed directions, unwilling to mark anyone attracting that much attention.

Saved by the screaming two-year-old.

Ben moved three feet forward. Thunder rolled overhead, and outside the shop windows, rain began to pour down on the pavement.

Why had he picked London in winter?

Oh right. Gold and notoriety.

The gold hoard of Brennus the Celt was a tale draped in shadows and wrapped in myth. It was an urban legend among *vampires*, for heaven's sake. A legendary treasure of weapons and gold artifacts so beautiful that Viking invaders wept at the sight of it, which was what gave Brennus time to kill them and hide his treasure.

According to the rumors.

But no one knew what had happened to Brennus, ancient immortal chieftain of Britain, much less his treasure. Everyone had stopped looking for traces of him or it a thousand years before. That chapter of history had drifted into legends. Searching for the treasure was a dead end. If no enterprising vampire had found it in twelve hundred years, then it was lost to history.

Ben wasn't buying it.

He finally made it to the front of the line and swiped his card for his dinner and beer. He left the market and turned left, heading toward the quiet house on Oxford Gardens.

The house wasn't noteworthy in any way. Just another rental house on a street of nearly identical row houses. It had three stories and a back garden. It was close to a tube station. It was anonymous and nowhere near most immortal neighborhoods, which was exactly the reason he liked it.

Half the owners on the street were part-time residents or in a constant state of refurbishment, which meant no one paid attention to the dark-haired American man who came and went at odd hours of the day and night.

Ben unlocked the heavy door and walked to the kitchen. He put the korma on the counter and the beer in the fridge. Then he went back to the entryway to kick off his shoes and peel off his damp overcoat. Clad in stocking feet and already feeling lighter, Ben returned to the kitchen and opened a beer.

Despite the disappointing news from the cartographer today, he was certain the treasure existed.

Ben had asked questions. Dropped hints. Listened to stories. Then he went where vampire treasure hunters didn't think to go. He looked in the human world. The tedious, daylit human world. He didn't look for a big treasure. He looked for one artifact. A weapon of such renown that it had been given a name by the Romans who encountered it.

Sanguine Raptor.

Ancient writers called it the Blood Thief.

It was Brennus's blade. The sword that slew thousands. Which might or might not be true. Ben was sure the sword existed, and he wanted it. He wanted that sword and the treasure that came with it. If he and Tenzin could find the treasure of Brennus the Celt, *they* would be the legends.

He'd found veiled mention of the sword in Tacitus's account of Agricola's governance of Britannia. He'd found another reference from a monk who'd traveled to Charlemagne's court just prior to the raid of Lindisfarne.

He popped the tray of korma into the microwave oven and leaned against the counter, drinking his ale and staring at the dark sway of damp trees in the back garden.

The Sanguine Raptor existed. The treasure existed. Ben had even narrowed down the geographical area based on recorded Viking raids in the north and had several probable sites to start hunting.

He just needed that one thing.

One clue. One mention. One... anything that pointed him to its hiding place. He was hoping Tywyll, the oldest vampire in the British Isles, would be the one to give him that key.

He squinted as he watched the trees. Why were they moving so much? He set his beer down and walked to the garden door. The rain had stopped and it wasn't windy. In fact, he hadn't noticed any breeze when he...

A dark figure jumped from the tree just as he opened the door. His heart leapt and his stomach dropped.

"It's you." He let out a breath.

Tenzin grinned. "Did you miss me?"

The ugly knot of frustration loosened in his chest. "Yes." He pulled her into a tight hug. "What took you so long?"

"I had things to do." She squeezed him back before she ducked under his arm and into the kitchen. "What smells so *—Why are you eating food from a microwave?*"

He followed her back in the house. "Because you haven't been here to cook for me."

She picked up the box and gave him a dirty look. "This is poison."

He smiled. "I really don't think it is."

"What is wrong with you?"

"Did you put holes in my ceiling?" He rubbed his eyes, suddenly exhausted. "I expected the walls, but the ceiling?"

She narrowed her eyes and started opening cupboards. "Don't try to change the subject. Now sit down. You have rice and lentils at least. I should be able to throw something together."

She kept muttering as she looked in the refrigerator and grabbed the one nod to fresh food he'd managed in London, a bag of mini carrots. Ben watched her bang around the kitchen, a smile on his face. The knots in his shoulders relaxed.

Tenzin was here.

Everything would be fine.

DESPITE THE STATE of his pantry, Tenzin managed to put together a pilaf dish that would make most people weep. And while she cooked, he pulled out all the research he'd put together and spread it on the table in the dining room. The journals and pictures. The property records and satellite pictures. As she cooked, he prepared to make his case.

"Tell me," she said, setting down two bowls of pilaf and grabbing the chair next to him.

"Brennus the Celt," Ben said.

"Didn't know him." Tenzin picked at her pilaf. "He was Carwyn's grandsire. Carwyn's mother, Maelona, was rumored to be the only surviving child of Brennus. She walked into the dawn almost a thousand years ago."

"But no one knows what happened to Brennus."

She shook her head. "Just rumors."

"And Brennus was rumored to have treasure stolen from the Romans. Welsh gold. Silver. Jewels and weapons."

Tenzin nodded slowly. "I have heard of this treasure."

Ben walked to the kitchen and grabbed his bottle of ale and another one for Tenzin. "Reports said that northern raiders were so in awe of Brennus's wealth that they were struck dumb at the sight of it." He walked back and handed her the beer before he sat again.

"Cheers." Tenzin tipped up her ale and drank. "And while the raiders were gaping, Brennus killed them. Chopped off their heads with his mighty blade."

"Yes. Now, before you start telling me it's a—"

"Legend. It's a legend." She shrugged. "Vampires have lots of legends, Ben. We get bored. We enjoy lying. We enjoy conning others of our kind when we can. It makes us feel superior."

"But Brennus's treasure wasn't *just* a legend. It existed at one time. Look." He shoved the journals to her. "The wealth of the chieftain Brennus was mentioned twice by Tacitus." He showed her another scan from the monk in the French court. "And in France by this priest. It was mentioned by multiple sources, not just one. Add to that the rumors in the immortal world and you have enough smoke that the fire has to exist."

She still looked skeptical.

Ben said, "Brennus's treasure existed."

"I agree, but that doesn't mean it *still* exists."

"I don't think it's been found and broken up. A gold hoard of that size would have been noted."

"Unless it was found by another vampire. We tend to keep quiet when we find lots of money."

"True, but—"

"And it might not be as big as you think. You have to remember, my Benjamin. Treasure in ancient Britain wasn't like treasure in the more civilized world. Brennus was a chieftain, not an emperor. He wouldn't have had a giant room filled with riches."

"Why not? Those did exist."

"But not *here*. Rome took most of Britain's gold." She looked out at the dark trees behind the house. "They took it far, far away. The gold Brennus was rumored to have might have been a single chest. It might have been next to nothing that he boasted of to make his enemies jealous."

"Was the Sanguine Raptor made up?"

Her eyes sharpened. "No. If any part of that legend is true, it's the Sanguine Raptor. I've heard too many details to doubt that. Rumors of it traveled all the way to Rome."

"What have you heard?"

"A Celtic blade made of the particular kind of iron Brennus had perfected. Very strong. Very flexible. Jeweled hilt."

"What style?"

"More a saber than a long sword. I'm not certain of that, but reports say that it was short—closer to the Roman gladius—and curved. Brennus forged his own iron. Earth vampire, remember?"

"So if the Sanguine Raptor existed, why not the rest of the treasure? According to legends—"

"Listen to yourself, Ben. *According to legends.*"

"Legends come from somewhere!"

She paused. "You're not wrong. All I'm saying is that *if* this treasure exists, it might not be on the grand scale it's made out to be. Is this really worth our time?"

Ben shuffled his papers together. He didn't need to convince Tenzin the treasure existed. After the past couple of summers, she owed him a job or two on faith. But Tenzin was a magpie and didn't like parting with her money. She also didn't like being bored. What he needed to do was convince her that looking for Brennus's hoard was worth the effort.

"This job, Tiny... You need to think bigger. It doesn't matter if it's *monetarily* worth it."

"Money always matters."

He folded his photos back into his notebook. "I'm thinking about reputation."

She grinned, her clawlike fangs glinting from the corner of her mouth. "I don't think my reputation needs any work."

He put everything in his folder and closed it. "Well, mine does. I'm willing to lose money on this deal if it means my reputation gets a boost. And you might not be as reputable as you think you are."

She snorted.

"Face it," he said. "Right now you're known as an assassin more than an antiquities hunter. People would hire you in a heartbeat to get rid of their enemies, but they're not necessarily going to trust you with the family silver."

"Which they shouldn't." She leaned forward. "Because I would keep it all for myself if you let me."

"Which is why I need to build *my* reputation if we're going to be partners. If we finish this job—"

"Did someone hire you for this or did you come up with this idea yourself?"

He sat back. "Finding a client is part of the job."

"You want to find a client to hire you to find a treasure you have already picked out?" Tenzin rested her chin on her hand. "Benjamin, I'm not sure you understand what contract work is about."

"We *need* to do this, Tiny."

"Says who?"

"Me. You agreed to be partners."

"Yes, I did. But Brennus's gold is the definition of a wild-goose chase. Hundreds of vampires have looked for this treasure. Hundreds. Why do you think you can find it?"

"Satellite photos, human resources, and metal detectors."

Tenzin stared at him, then she threw her head back and started laughing.

SHE WASN'T LAUGHING at him. Not really.

Okay, maybe a little.

She was laughing more at his ego. Her Benjamin was bold.

"Satellite photos, human resources, and metal detectors."

Confidence had never been a problem for Ben.

"Fine." He glared at her as she wiped her eyes. "Laugh. But you're going to do this for me, Tiny."

How long would it take to talk him out of this crazy scheme? And was there anything she wanted to do before she returned to New York? She'd already visited the Harry Potter studio. She'd visited the ravens at the Tower. There wasn't much else—

"Are you listening?" he asked. "You're staying and you're helping me because you owe me."

She frowned. "What do I owe you for?"

He held up his hand. "Xinjiang." One finger. "Shanghai." Two fingers. "The freighter." Five fingers went up.

"That was years ago."

He held up his other hand. "Naples. Running for my life in Venice. Filomena."

"Hey! You walked into that one all on your own."

"Breaking into Hogwarts?"

He sure had a lot of fingers held up.

"I didn't ask you to come and get me from Hogwarts,"

Tenzin said. "I could have avoided those guards on my own."

"And I'm not even going to count the raccoon thing."

She pointed at him. "Raccoons are assholes. You know it. I know it. The whole world knows it."

"Fine." He picked up his beer. "But you owe me."

"But—"

"Don't even think about arguing," he said. "You're going to help me, Tenzin. Or..."

"Or what?" This ought to be good. She crossed her arms and waited for his worst.

Ben smiled. "I'll tell Giovanni you were the one who deleted his recording of the *King of Iron Chefs* 'Chen versus Sakai' battle."

Her smile almost fell. "You wouldn't."

His raised eyebrow said he would. Ben could be cunning when he put his mind to it.

"And the Chinese cabbage battle."

Tenzin's eyes went wide.

"Didn't know I knew about that one, did you?"

"I admit nothing."

Ben shrugged. "Doesn't matter when he already suspects you."

"Both those episodes are on YouTube!" she snarled. "He's just being stubborn."

"You know he hates watching TV on the computer."

Tenzin glared at him and stood. Damn conniving human.

She was so proud.

And irritated.

"You're going to help me," Ben said. "I'm meeting with Gemma tomorrow night. Now that you're here, I'm going to request a meeting with Tywyll."

She curled her lip. "That old man?"

"Is he any older than you?"

"I have no idea. Probably not." She was pouting. She knew it. Tenzin hated when Ben bested her.

Damn that *Iron Chef Japan* and its improbably entertaining kitchen battles.

Ben said, "Tywyll was a contemporary of Brennus. According to Carwyn, he was in Cornwall when Brennus was in southern Scotland, but they wrote to each other regularly and Tywyll considers him a friend."

"Considers? As in presently?"

"That's the other thing. According to Terrance Ramsay, Tywyll thinks Brennus is just hiding."

"Tywyll thinks Brennus is alive?"

"Yes."

Tenzin rolled her eyes. "Yes, he sounds like a brilliant source. Highly reliable."

"To be fair, no one witnessed Brennus's death or even heard rumors of it. It was always assumed that he burned up somewhere because he disappeared, but there's not any evidence of it. It's possible he's hiding. Haven't you ever hidden from the world?"

"I think my maximum was around a thousand years." She squinted. "Maybe two."

Ben opened his laptop again. "Well, Brennus has only been missing for twelve hundred, so it's entirely poss— Wait. Why are you smiling now?"

"I was just thinking that stealing treasure from a hidden vampire is much more entertaining than finding lost treasure from a dead one."

He shook his head. "You're twisted."

"You knew that already." She stood and cleared the dishes. "So when do you want to start?"

2

B EN WOULD LIKE TO SAY that the Swan with Two Necks lived up to its name.

It didn't.

"This place is a dump," Tenzin said.

"I'm sure its regulars think it's delightful, so try not to share that sentiment too loudly."

"Fine." She whispered, "This place is a dump."

He smiled and hooked an arm around her neck. "Come on. The old man said he'd meet us inside."

The floating pub creaked when they stepped aboard. Then it creaked when Ben opened the door. In fact, Ben had a hard time imagining how the building remained afloat unless Tywyll kept it held together by the sheer force of his amnis.

Which, according to his aunt, was entirely possible.

Tywyll was a water vampire who could easily be as old as Tenzin, if not older. His reputation left everything to the imagination. He was a loner. He was not ambitious. But the River Thames was *his water*. And not a single vampire in

England—not even Terrance Ramsay—disputed Tywyll's claim on it. Ever.

He was sitting in a booth when they walked in. Ben knew it was him because every other eye in the place turned toward them, glanced, then nodded toward the back corner booth. They walked toward the small man with pale skin. He was dark-haired and his face was lined. Tywyll wore the uniform of a man who worked on the river. Sturdy pants. Worn shirt fraying at the collar. Heavy shoes. Flat tweed cap.

But his energy crackled. Ben knew he was approaching one of the most powerful vampires in Britain. What he wasn't sure of—what no one was sure of—was whether Tywyll would be a friend or enemy that night.

The vampire looked up as they approached and nodded toward the opposite bench. "Ye'd be Vecchio's lad then."

"I am." Ben thought about holding out his hand but didn't. He made sure his pulse was steady and his breathing even.

Tywyll turned his eyes on Tenzin. "And I'd bet my pint on ye being the windwalker."

"You wouldn't be wrong," Tenzin said.

"What're ye doin' with this 'un?" Tywyll nodded at Ben. "He's not yer sort."

"He's my sort if I say he is." Tenzin's eyes went cold. "Don't pretend you know me, old man."

Tywyll cackled. "Ye've as many years as me. Or maybe I have more. But fine. Say yer piece, young Vecchio."

Ben decided Tywyll would appreciate the direct approach best. This wasn't a vampire who wanted niceties and charm. "We're looking for the Sanguine Raptor," he said. "According to rumors, you and Brennus were contemporaries. Some say friends. Are they correct?"

Tywyll's eyes went sharp. "The Sanguine Raptor, you say? And what's that?"

Ben smiled. "Brennus's sword. A sword so famous Roman historians mentioned it. Are you saying you've never heard the name?"

"Ah." Tywyll took a long drink. "You'd be asking after the *Fitheach Lann* then."

"The what?"

"*Fitheach Lann*, boy. The raven blade," Tywyll said. "You're looking for Brennus's blade and you don't even know the name of it?"

Ben filed the information away. Some of his immortal sources had drawn parallels between the real vampire Brennus and the mythical figure of Bran the Blessed in Welsh mythology. Bran, "the Giant King." The *Raven* King. In addition to the name similarities, the Sanguine Raptor was depicted as a curved Roman-era blade that resembled a *falcata*. More important to Tywyll's leading questions was the hilt, which was drawn as a stylized raven with ruby eyes.

"Forgive us, Tywyll. You're correct. The *Fitheach Lann* sounds like the sword we're looking for."

Tywyll narrowed his eyes. "And what greed possessed you to seek a sword not made for your hand?"

"We don't seek the Sanguine Raptor for ourselves. We've been hired to find it by someone in Brennus's line."

"Is that so?" Tywyll said. "And who'd be that 'un?"

Ben said, "That's between me and my client. We haven't been given permission to share that information. Not even with you."

"Ye've the look of truth. Or maybe the look of a good liar." Tywyll nodded and took a long swallow of his ale. "You don't have permission to say who seeks the sword. And Brennus didn't give me permission to share where he buried the *Fitheach Lann*, so I suppose we're at an impasse, ain't we?"

His uncle had said that Tywyll liked to play games, so Ben smiled. After all, games were supposed to be fun.

"So you know where it is?" Ben asked.

"Did I say that?"

"You implied it."

Tywyll's eyes glinted. "I might 'ave. Doesn't change that Brennus ne'er gave me leave to share that piece with you." He took another drink. "Not that ye'd be the first to ask about Brennus in the now and lately."

"Really?" Tenzin leaned forward, resting her elbow on the table. "Who else has been asking about Brennus?"

"Folks here and there," Tywyll said. "Been folks askin' about Brennus for centuries now."

Asking about Brennus, but what about Bran? Both were legends, but if the Sanguine Raptor belonged to Brennus, then the *Fitheach Lann* belonged to Bran.

"They're asking the wrong questions," Ben said.

Tywyll's eyes narrowed. "Are they?"

"They ask about his treasure, but do they spare a song for the Raven King?"

"Few do." Tywyll's eyes met Ben's and he smiled a little. "But humble folk still be hanging ribbons at the Raven King's tree."

"Is that so?" Humble could mean poor. But Tywyll was ancient, and in Middle English, humble meant "low to the ground." Were "humble folk" people of the earth? Mortals?

Humans were hanging ribbons at the Raven King's tree.

"Many looked for favor that way," Tywyll said. "Though only the wise'll find it. Brennus never put stock in trinkets and tricks. Not like the one come looking."

Tenzin pressed. "When?"

"Fortnight past." Tywyll took another long drink. "But he didn't have a coin for the new king's stone."

Trees and ribbons. Stones and kings.

Ben kept the smile contained. Barely. He didn't know if his pulse gave him away. Tywyll had given him the key, but he had to remain calm.

"That was foolish," Ben said. "You should always bring a coin for the Raven King's throne."

Tywyll cocked his head. "Ravens like ribbons, but they like silver more."

"I can hang a ribbon at the Raven's tree," Ben said, "But I'm happy to pass a coin to the riverman first."

"A coin for the river will never serve you wrong." Tywyll's eyes twinkled. "But save your silver for the king, young Vecchio. Do ye think ye know where yer headed then?"

Ben let the smile break through. "I do."

"We'll see if yer as keen as your auntie, won't we? She's a great one for a riddle."

"How about the other one who came asking?" Ben asked. "Did he like riddles?"

"The other liked flash and fire. Blood of the Raven, but none of the ken."

"Blood of the Raven?"

Tywyll nodded slowly. "Watch yerself, young Vecchio. Yer not the only one digging into the past."

Tenzin's eyes darted back and forth between the two of them. "Okay," she said, nodding. "Ben, I'm going to get a beer. Do you want one?"

He smiled. "Sure. Tywyll, what'll you have?"

"Another porter," the old man said. "Then ye can tell me all about how yer lovely auntie is faring out in California with that fire-starter she mated."

≈

"BENJAMIN!" Gemma Melcombe, earth vampire and first lady of London immortal society, strode into the sitting room, hands held out. "I've been hoping you would make time to see me."

She was tall for her era, pale-skinned and blond with vivid blue eyes. No matter what Gemma was wearing, Ben imagined her dressed for a period film. She was the child of Carwyn ap Bryn, who was like another uncle to Ben. He'd already tried to mine Carwyn for information about Brennus, but the jovial immortal had been surprisingly tight-lipped. Ben was hoping Gemma would be more forthcoming.

"Gemma." Ben stood and kissed both her cheeks. "Thank you for meeting us. I'm sorry I didn't come around sooner."

At one point, Gemma had also been his uncle's lover. Ben thanked the heavens daily that hadn't lasted. He wasn't nearly fancy enough to be Gemma's adopted son.

Tenzin remained seated, paging through a coffee table book. "Hello, Gemma."

"Tenzin." Luckily, Gemma seemed amused, not offended. "Welcome to you as well."

Tenzin slammed the book shut and looked around the room. "You have opinions on decorating."

Ben thought he ought to be concerned about Tenzin's line of questioning, but he was too curious where it might be leading.

"I do," Gemma said, settling on the settee across from Tenzin. "I've been to several design schools. It's a fascinating subject, and of course, with our color perception being what it is, subtleties are easier for us to recognize. I heard you and Ben have a new place in Manhattan." She glanced at him. "What neighborhood?"

"SoHo." He sat down next to Tenzin. "We have a penthouse loft on Mercer. Built late nineteenth century. Great ironwork."

"And very tall ceilings," Tenzin added. "With roof access. I want to make a garden there."

Ben said, "You didn't tell me you wanted a garden."

"Well, I do."

Gemma said, "I'd love to see it. Is it renovated?"

"It was an artist's loft," Ben said. "The rest of the building was renovated a few years ago, but our seller used it as a gallery. So it's mostly empty, but the walls are in good shape. One bathroom. A little kitchen. The wood floors are redone. We have the floor below for our office and storage."

Gemma said, "It sounds like a wonderful space."

"But how should I hang my swords?" Tenzin said, looking intently at Gemma. "Should I try for something symmetrical or more utilitarian?"

Gemma seemed stymied by that one, but only for a minute. "I'd aim for eclectic but balanced. Have you thought about mixing art in with the weapons? I'm assuming your collection is drawn from several eras."

Tenzin leaned forward. "It is! And various martial traditions. Mixed metals as well."

"Then mixing the weapons with the art will create a gallery effect for the space." She glanced at Ben. "And also make the collection appear a bit more... decorative than functional."

In other words, mix art in with the sabers, or human company might get weirded out.

Thank you, Gemma.

Tenzin smiled and leaned back on the settee. "See? I

knew she'd be the right person to ask. The television shows never talk about the right things."

The look on Gemma's face was Ben's signal to change the subject. "How are things, Gemma? I met with Terry last week, and he said the stuff going down in Athens has been... interesting."

She raised a delicate eyebrow. "It's definitely a shift in power. And lower risk for Elixir poisoning could affect the blood-wine market, but we'll see. Vampires are cautious. So far, orders don't seem to be falling off."

Tenzin elbowed Ben. "Remind me to order some before we leave."

He frowned. "You barely feed as it is. You need blood-wine?"

Her teeth glinted in the lamplight. "No, I just like the taste."

Ben managed not to shudder. Blood-wine was exactly what it sounded like. Blood preserved in wine. The preservation process Gemma and Terry's winemaker had perfected served two purposes. It preserved blood for years without cold or anticoagulants, and it removed any trace of Elixir—a deadly vampire virus—from the blood supply. The good news was, reports from the Mediterranean indicated that Elixir was probably on the way out in the vampire world. This time for good.

Gemma asked, "How are Giovanni and Beatrice, Ben? I haven't been to the West Coast in years. And they seem to be hermits these days."

"They like their books," he said. "Unless I drag them to Italy, they're usually in Los Angeles or Chile. The quiet life suits them."

"Indeed." Gemma glanced over as a maid set down a tray with cordial glasses and two dark bottles. "Tenzin, would you like to try some of our new blood-port? And Ben, I've brought out the non-blood variety as well."

"Yes, please." Tenzin held out her hand as Gemma poured. "Ben, when are you going to ask her the real question?"

The corner of Gemma's mouth turned up. "You mean you didn't come here to talk about design ideas and try my new wine? I'm shocked."

"I came for that," Tenzin said. "He's the one with ulterior motives."

With a single look from their mistress, the humans standing in the corners of the room left, leaving Gemma alone with Ben and Tenzin. "Does this have something to do with your research in Exeter and the reason you wanted to speak to Tywyll? You've attracted some attention from certain quarters, Ben. I hope that's not a surprise."

"It's not. And yes, that's why I'm here." He wasn't surprised that Gemma knew about Exeter. He was a friend, but he was still a human under a foreign vampire's aegis who was traveling within Gemma's territory. "But my research project has something to do with your family as well."

Gemma looked less bored and more interested. "Is that so?"

"You know that Tenzin and I have started our own offshoot of Gio's business, right?"

"Hunting antiquities, I believe." Gemma spread her hands. "I wish I had a job for you, but right now I don't. If I need your services in the future, you can be sure I'll contact you."

"I appreciate that, but right now we're in the middle of a job. That's what the research in Exeter is about."

"Old land maps, Benjamin?" Gemma sipped her port.

"One would almost think you're involved in *treasure* hunting."

"And get my hands dirty?" Ben winked at her. "Come on, Gemma. You know I'm a city boy."

"You think you fool me with your charm and wit," Gemma said. "And I'll let you continue the illusion. But don't forget, Benjamin Vecchio." Gemma glanced at Tenzin. "Like recognizes like."

He sighed dramatically. "Why must you think the worst of me?"

Gemma laughed. "Why do you think it's the worst? Don't forget who my mate is."

A barely reformed criminal, Ben thought. If anyone knew what it meant to tread the line between dark and light, it was Terrance Ramsay. Gemma pulled Terry over to the side of the good guys... most of the time.

"I'm hunting something," Ben said. "A sword."

"Oh?" Gemma's eyes flashed with something Ben didn't catch. "What sword?"

"The Sanguine Raptor."

Her mouth firmed into a line. "Do you like your life, Benjamin?"

"I'm a pretty big fan of it, yeah."

Her eyebrows rose. "Then quietly return whatever money you've been given, apologize to your client, and go home."

That was *not* the response he'd been hoping for. Tenzin sat still and silent at his side.

Ben shook his head. "That's not the way it works."

She said, "Brennus's treasure is not something to play with."

"So you're not going to try to convince me it doesn't exist?"

"No," Gemma said. "I'm going to tell you that searching for it could be your end."

Tenzin took a sip of her port. "That's excellent," she said. "A little too sweet for my taste, but it's very good." She stared at Gemma for a few more moments before she said, "Ben, we should be going."

Ben frowned. "What? We haven't asked her—"

"We should go," Tenzin said again. "Thank you, Gemma."

Gemma nodded. "Tenzin."

Tenzin stood and looked down at Ben. He felt his temper rise; he turned to Gemma. "Blood of the Raven," he said. "Tywyll mentioned the blood of the Raven was looking for the treasure. Brennus was the Raven King. You, your brothers, all of Carwyn's family are the blood of the Raven. Is that why you're shutting me out? Has someone in your family been asking about Brennus's sword?"

Gemma rose, and Ben was forced by drilled-in manners to rise with her.

"I'm sorry," she said graciously. "I don't know anything about that."

"Really? You don't know if anyone in your family has been in town asking about your great-grandsire's treasure?"

Tenzin pulled on his arm. "Thank you, Gemma. Good-bye. Thank you again for the wine. I'll send a messenger with my order before we leave the city."

"Of course." Gemma leaned over and kissed both Ben's cheeks. "Ben, it was so good to see you. Please give Giovanni and Beatrice my regards."

"I'll make sure to do that." He was pissed. So, *so* pissed. Gemma knew something and she was holding back. Tenzin better have a damn good reason for retreating, or she had a lot to answer for.

"Ben."

Gemma called his name, and he turned at the door.

"Leave it alone. I'm asking you to leave it alone." She sighed. "Even though I can tell by the look in your eyes that you won't. You're too much like your uncle."

"I take comparisons to my uncle as a compliment, Gemma."

"You should. But you should also remember something else." She smiled sadly. "Giovanni is a fire vampire with a reputation earned over many centuries and many battles. I know he has taught you many things, Ben. But you are not your uncle. And you are so much easier to kill."

Without another word, Tenzin pulled him from the room.

USUALLY Tenzin left him when he started down the stairs to the underground, but that night she didn't. She followed him to the High Street Kensington station, pulling out her own Oyster card for the tube. Ben didn't even know she had an Oyster card. She walked with him silently as he followed the signs for the Circle Line and racked his brain.

Gemma knew something.

Blood of the Raven.

Brennus's line.

Did Carwyn have siblings?

How many children did Carwyn have?

How many children did *Carwyn's children* have?

The train pulled into the station and Ben boarded, Tenzin walking silently behind. It was nearly ten p.m., and they were the only travelers at their end of the compartment. He sat down and stared out the black windows as the doors hissed closed, and Tenzin took the seat next to him.

Just how much "blood of the Raven" was wandering around Western Europe? Had Tywyll given whoever this mystery person was the same information about the Raven King's tree? Had they also discovered the stones in Dunino Den?

"...he didn't have a coin for the new king's stone."

No, Ben didn't think Tywyll had given the key to the other seeker. Still, the question remained—

"So, who do you think it is?" Tenzin asked.

"I don't know," he said quietly. "But Gemma does."

"She won't tell us." Tenzin stretched out her legs and crossed her arms. "The only people Gemma cares about are family."

And Ben wasn't family.

"Tywyll said the other one had 'Raven's blood.' I assumed it was part of Carwyn's family. Are there any other descendants from Brennus's line?"

She shook her head. "If there are, they're hidden. Brennus did live on the Continent for many years. He was originally from the Celtic tribes in the Carpathian Basin. My sire's men had occasional conflicts with them. That was the first time I heard his name. He had other children, but as far as I know, they were all killed in a massive battle around two thousand years ago. It was rumored that was the reason he went to Britain. After that, there was only Maelona and her sister. I don't know the sister's name. Then from Maelona, Carwyn."

"So as far as anyone knows, all of Brennus's blood is concentrated in Carwyn's line?"

"Yes. And Gemma would only care about protecting her sire's clan. She has no love for anyone other than her family and her mate. She has friends—your uncle, for instance—but she'd sell Gio out in a minute for her own blood."

Ben mulled it over as the train hurtled under the city. They transferred at Edgeware Road and walked across the platform to catch the train to Ladbroke Grove.

"There's something else she's not telling us," he said.

"I know." Tenzin tapped her foot. She hated being underground. "I may be more worried about that than whoever is looking for the treasure. She warned you away from it, and Gemma isn't overly dramatic."

"You've known her for a long time."

She shrugged. "When she was still with Giovanni."

"Hmm."

Ben stared at the blurred rush of the train as it came to a stop in the station. They entered again, this time with more company, so Ben stood silently while Tenzin leaned against the front of the compartment. Black windows underground turned to grey night as they resurfaced past Paddington. The city glowed with passing streetlamps while raindrops made dancing jewels on the windows of the car.

He took Tenzin's hand when their station was called. Sometimes, when she wasn't thinking about it, she forgot to keep her feet on the ground. Tucking her under his arm, Ben walked down from the platform and steered them up the deserted street. The only fellow walkers that night were two drunk men and a lone dog trotting up the middle of the road. Tenzin walked silently with him as they turned left and ambled down their quiet street, but she halted when they reached the gate before their house.

"Someone is inside," she said under her breath.

Ben palmed the blade concealed in his coat lining and looked around. There were no eyes on them, so he jerked his chin up. Tenzin took off, flying up and over the house as he approached the front.

He was at the top step when he heard the whistling. Someone was in his house. And they were whistling.

The front door was unlocked. He pulled it open and walked into the dark entryway. The light was on in the kitchen and he smelled... tea?

A short scuffle, a loud bang, then he heard Tenzin say, "I've got him."

Ben walked back to the kitchen to see a dark-haired Caucasian man sitting at the kitchen table, a teacup halfway to his lips. Tenzin's blade was at his throat.

The stranger's smile was crooked and his eyes were dancing. "I was only trying to make myself comfortable until you returned."

The accent was undoubtedly French. The energy was vampire. Ben didn't say a word. He sat across from the man —the vampire—who'd been foolish enough to invade his and Tenzin's territory and set his hunting knife on the table. His pulse was low and steady.

"Allow me to introduce myself," the stranger said. "My name is René Dupont. And I do hope you won't tell Gemma I'm in town."

3

"**W**HO IS GEMMA TO YOU?" Ben asked.

René's eyes narrowed. "Who is she to *you?*"

"A friend," Tenzin said. "She's certainly never broken into our home. Ben, why don't you call Gemma now?"

A flash of concern in René's eyes when Ben pulled out his phone. "I wouldn't."

"Oh?" Ben asked. "Why not?"

"She won't thank you for it. My aunt has known I'm here for weeks. If she can deny it, she can leave me in peace. If she can't..."

"No offense, Frenchie, but your peace is not my problem." Ben unlocked his phone. Tenzin gripped René's hair and pulled his head back, exposing the slow pulse in his throat.

"We have a common interest!" René said.

"What's that?"

"The Sanguine Raptor."

Ben's eyes met Tenzin's. Her grip on the blade tightened, and a drop of blood spilled from René's neck. Ben held up a hand and her grip relaxed.

Slightly.

"What do you know about the Sanguine Raptor?" Ben asked.

"Not as much as you," René said, his eyes dancing again despite the blood that rolled down his neck to meet his collar. "I must confess, I was simply... curious at first, but now I'm quite fascinated. My father has spoken of Brennus's greatness for as long as I can remember. This is the first time I've actually been able to imagine the reality. Rumors are that you are close to finding it."

Ben shrugged. "So what? You think we want your help? You may not know this, René, but Tenzin and I do this—as in *professionally*. We're working for a client, and we don't need extra help."

René's face fell. His eyes were stricken. His shoulders slumped and Tenzin released her grip on his hair. She looked at Ben.

He rolled his eyes.

Tenzin dropped her sword and stood to the side, but her hand remained on René's shoulder.

Ben almost felt bad for snuffing out the vampire's excitement until René threw his head back and burst into laughter. His dark curls bounced around his head as he leapt to his feet and darted to the corner of the room. From the safety of his corner, René bit his lip and winked at Tenzin, who stood, her arms crossed, watching him with a blank expression.

"My dear human," René said with a smile. "Whyever do you think I would want to help *you*? I'm not going to help you find Brennus's hoard." His smile fell away. "I'm going to steal it."

...he didn't have a coin for the new king's stone.

So here was the one who put stock in trinkets and tricks.

Even with Tywyll's warning, René had surprised him. Ben had been spotting cons since he was a boy, but he'd lowered his guard once he knew René was in Carwyn's clan.

He was getting soft in friendly territory. He'd have to change that.

Ben decided to play along. "So you're going to steal it from us? And how are you going to do that, René?"

René cocked his head. "Well, you may not know this, Benjamin Vecchio, ward of the great assassin Giovanni Vecchio, but I do this. As in *professionally*."

"You're a professional thief?" That was a new one. Since when did thieves advertise? "I've never heard of you."

"If you had, I wouldn't be very good at my job, would I?" René turned to Tenzin and pressed his hands together in front of his chest. "But you, my lady Tenzin. Daughter of Penglai. Commander of the Altan Wind. *You...*" His eyes heated. "The honor you have given me by marking my neck humbles me. I am at a loss for how I can repay you."

Tenzin frowned. "Are you trying to flatter me?"

"Flattery would be dishonest, while I speak only the truth."

Oh brother... Ben tried not to roll his eyes. "So you think you're going to steal the treasure from us?"

"Oh no. I know I will." René was still staring at Tenzin, and a smile teased the corner of his mouth. "Lady Tenzin, your human is impertinent."

Tenzin smiled, and her clawlike fangs became visible. "He is not my human."

René sucked in a breath. "Beautiful."

"Lethal."

"Is there a difference?" René's gaze swung back to Ben, and feigned merriment turned to swift calculation. "So he is not your human? I understand."

"I very much doubt that," Tenzin said. "Ben is my partner. I am not looking for another. You may leave now." Tenzin cocked her head. "But perhaps it is too late for that."

René's eyes narrowed and darted toward the entryway a second before Gemma roared into the house, her appearance causing the foundation to tremble beneath him.

René showed his first real emotion in the very odd night.

"Oh damn." He grimaced. "Good evening, Gemma."

GEMMA Melcombe was *SEETHING*.

"You will get out of England, René. You will leave tonight and you will not come back."

René spread his hands in a pacifying gesture. "*Ma tante*, you are overreacting."

Ben and Tenzin were watching the show playing out in the living room. Ben started a fire and decided this was the best entertainment he'd seen in weeks. Tenzin grabbed two beers and handed one to him before she perched on the back of his armchair.

"You think this is overreacting?" Gemma's face was colder and more vicious than Ben had ever seen it. And the first immortal lady of London was regularly referred to as the Ice Queen. "I intervened for you years ago, René. You were a foolish boy then, and you're a foolish boy now. Nothing has changed."

Ben whispered, "What did he do?"

Tenzin said, "I'm not sure."

Gemma whirled on them. "You want to know what he did? He aided in the death of Terry's sire and *my friend*. He was part of a coup—"

"I didn't know they were planning those things!" René shouted. "For pity's sake, Gem—"

"You will get no more pity from me!" She bared her fangs. "It was unwitting. *Fine*. But isn't that typical? You bounce around the world, charming your way in and out of trouble. Leaving the most horrendous wake as you sail past the little people who are forced to clean up after you. Is that what Guy would want for you, René? Your father—"

"My father doesn't give a damn about me," René snarled. "He wishes he'd never turned me. He said so himself."

"Grow up." Gemma practically spat out the words. "He's tired of your antics. Just as we all are. Find something useful to do with your eternity. Then maybe your father will speak to you again."

Tenzin handed Ben a bowl of popcorn that seemed to appear out of nowhere.

"Where did you get this?" he whispered.

"Shhhhh."

"You're leaving tonight," Gemma said. She glanced at the clock over the mantel. "You have eight hours to get your affairs together, but you're leaving our territory *tonight*."

René kicked up his feet on the coffee table, and Ben kicked them off again.

The Frenchman glared and said, "I'm not going anywhere. I'm not afraid of Terrance Ramsay."

Tenzin snorted and beer sprayed through her hand.

"Gross," Ben said.

"He's not afraid of Terry," Tenzin said. "That's funny."

René said, "And I am not afraid of you either, Gemma. You may cluck like an angry hen, but at the end of the day, I am your blood." He shot an arrogant look at Ben. "You will not sell me out for these two."

"I don't care one damn about these two," Gemma said. "But if you think I'm going to let my mate deal with you, you're very much mistaken." Her voice dripped scorn. "Terry *will* kill you, René. Because Terry keeps his promises. He'll kill you, and then he will hurt. He will feel regret. Sorrow. Not for you, but for *me*. For your father."

René narrowed his eyes.

"Do you think I'm going to let that happen?" Gemma's voice dropped to a whisper. "Do you think my loyalty to *you* will allow me to let my mate hurt?" She bent over his shoulder. "I will kill you myself, little boy, before Terry ever sees your face. I will kill you so he doesn't have to. You have eight hours, René. Make the most of them."

René's eyes locked with Benjamin's. His eyes narrowed and he pursed his lips in a sneering kiss.

Then—in a blink—he was gone.

Ben heard the night wind gusting down the hallway as the old oak door squeaked on its hinges.

SHE STARED AT THE FIRE, sipping the glass of wine Tenzin had poured for her.

"He's incurably charming," Gemma said. "That's most of his problem. He's also very smart and very capable."

"Is that why you followed us?" Ben asked. He hadn't noticed a tail.

"I *had* you followed, Ben. You'll be happy to know I made sure to put one of Terry's best men on it. I wouldn't want to insult you."

"Fine. Why did you have us followed?"

"Because René likes to play with his prey. It's as simple and as complicated as that."

Arrogant, interfering vampires.

"What does he do?" Tenzin said.

"He's a thief. More or less. A gambler." She sighed. "René is whatever he wants to be when he wants to be it."

"He's a hustler," Ben said. He knew René's kind. His mother *was* René's kind.

"Yes, he is." Gemma gave him a wry smile. "So is my husband, if we're being honest. The difference is, René doesn't care who he hurts along the way. And he's much more comfortable lying."

Ben asked, "What does he know about Brennus's treasure?"

Gemma took a deep breath and paused. She looked at Ben. Then Tenzin. Then back to Ben. "You won't leave this alone, will you?"

"No," he said. "Especially not now."

"Your research has attracted attention," Gemma said. "That's the only reason René is here. I don't know who hired him, but he'll have a client. He doesn't hunt for the sake of hunting."

Ben leaned forward, his elbows propped on his knees. "How much do you think he knows?"

"If I were a gambler... I would bet that René knows as much about Brennus's treasure as you do. I made inquiries after Tywyll brought it to my attention. He's been in London for weeks."

But he didn't give a coin to the riverman.

René didn't know what Tywyll had told them. That was Ben's bet. And Ben was a pretty decent gambler himself.

But Ben hadn't counted on someone shadowing his steps. René could easily have followed Ben's movements. He might know what offices and universities he'd visited.

What books he'd borrowed. What experts he'd interviewed. With the proper use of amnis, René could get a fairly clear idea of Ben's movements so far.

Of course, René was also limited by daylight, so Ben had that to his advantage.

"Whatever you have planned," Gemma said, "I want no part of it. I have too much happening in my own city to seek drama elsewhere. My one word of advice is this: René—whether you like it or not—carries Brennus's blood. If you find anything and he can make a claim that supersedes yours, no vampire will be on your side, Benjamin. You're human. And your partner is from the East."

Ben said, "So hire me to find it for you. I promise my terms are very reasonable."

She raised her hands, palms out. "Not even for Giovanni's son. I refuse to involve myself in this, and I don't want you bothering my father either. Carwyn has more than enough to worry about at the moment."

He'd already interviewed Carwyn, who had been less than forthcoming and quickly changed the subject to far more entertaining things than treasure. The old earth vampire was good at that. Ben would go visit him for one reason and quickly find himself in the middle of some lunacy that had nothing to do with the original purpose of his visit.

One Christmas Ben had ended up herding sheep in nothing but his underwear. He still wasn't quite sure how that had happened. "Listen, Gemma—"

"*Don't* bother Carwyn," she said again. "However..."

Gemma seemed to deliberate again.

Come on, you know you want to help me.

Finally she said, "If you happen to head north..." She

gave him a loaded look. "I imagine Max and Cathy would love to meet you."

Yes!

"Oh?" he said, trying to keep his heart rate steady.

"If you happened to be in Edinburgh," Gemma said. "I'm sure I could call."

Well, it appeared that Gemma knew far more about Brennus's hoard than she'd let on. And René must have really pissed her off.

Ben couldn't stop his smile. "I would *love* to meet Max and Cathy."

"It would only be polite," she said. "Considering your... ongoing connections to our family."

Score. Max was one of Carwyn's sons, and Cathy was Max's mate. She was also a fire vampire and chief of security in Edinburgh. Ben had been going to ask for an introduction anyway, but Gemma calling ahead more than took care of any political hoops. More importantly, if Ben could convince Max to hire them, he'd be in the clear over any claims René might make. Max was a generation closer to Brennus and would have a greater claim on any recovered artifacts.

"So Scotland?" Ben tried to look innocent. "What a lovely idea. I love Scottish weather in the fall."

Tenzin frowned. "Why?"

Ben slid from his chair and scooted over to Gemma, taking her hand and kissing it. "You're a peach, Gemma Melcombe. And no talk of bloody retribution will convince me otherwise. A *peach*."

Gemma rolled her eyes. "God save me from charming men."

≈

Edinburgh, Scotland

THE ROLLICKING THUMP of Scottish punk filled the pub where Ben and Tenzin dodged drunken festivalgoers fleeing the more traditional concerts that filled the city during the Scots Fiddle Festival. Bagpipes clashed with electric guitars. A singer wailed into the microphone as drums crashed in the corner.

"I love this!" Tenzin yelled, earplugs stuck in her ears. He'd forced them on her a block from the pub.

"I'm glad!"

"I can't hear you!"

"I can't imagine why!"

He grabbed her arm after they'd procured two pints from the bar and made their way down a long hallway where the music was still clear, but less demanding. Max and Cathy sat canoodling in a corner booth.

Yep. Ben was pretty sure that was the word for it. Canoodling.

Tenzin stopped. "I'm judging them."

"Just because you're not a fan of public displays of affection doesn't mean they can't be."

"He looks like he's devouring her face. That can't be pleasant."

"Will you stop?" He tugged her hand. "I'm sure they'll cease and desist when we sit down."

Except they didn't. Or... not right away.

Cathy eventually came up for air. Ben could feel the heat of her skin from his seat across the booth.

"Sorry. Max has just come into town tonight. We haven't seen each other in four weeks."

Ben said, "If tonight's not a good night, we can—"

"It's fine," Max said, his voice rough as he pressed kisses

45

along Cathy's neck. "It's very nice to meet you, Ben. Tenzin, you too."

"I don't feel like we've actually met yet," Tenzin said. "Though I feel that I'm well acquainted with your mate's breasts."

Max lifted his head and looked at the hand resting under Cathy's sweater. "Oh. Sorry about that."

"I'm not," Cathy said. Luckily, she straightened her sweater anyway and faced them.

"Oh," Tenzin said. "You both have faces. Imagine that."

"Is she always this way?" Cathy said.

"Yes." Ben took a drink.

Cathy smiled. "Cool!"

Ben continued, "So Max, I've heard a lot about you. All of it is good."

"Well, that's nice to hear."

Ben said, "And Cathy, apparently you're a raging she-beast who will devour me and destroy my sense of dignity if I allow it."

"Ah!" Cathy said. "You've been talking to Deirdre then."

"How did you know?"

Cathy laughed and laid her head on Max's shoulder. "I love your sister, Max."

"It's to your credit that you haven't wiped her from exis-tence, darling."

"I'm sure you tell her the same thing."

"Of course I do."

Tenzin looked back and forth between Cathy and Max as if she were watching tennis. "I like you. Well, now that you're not showing me your tongues. I found that episode rather disgusting."

"Thanks," Cathy said. "I'm not sure how I feel about you." She leaned forward. "Are your fangs always down?"

Tenzin leaned forward too. "Yes."

"How do you eat?"

"I suppose like everyone else. I don't remember *not* having my fangs down, so I don't know any other way."

Cathy frowned. "Fascinating. Can I ask how you—?"

"No." Max pulled Cathy back. "No, you cannot."

"You don't know what I was going to ask," Cathy protested.

"Yes, I do." He cleared his throat. "So, Ben, what did you want to talk to me about?"

Ben said, "You changed the subject so gracefully I barely noticed."

Max smiled. "Thanks."

"I sense they both have boundary issues."

"I heard you were a young man of sense"—the vampire finished his whisky—"and it appears the rumors were correct."

Max was one of the most human vampires Ben had ever seen. From his dress to his mannerisms, he struck Ben as a thoroughly well-adjusted immortal. All of Carwyn's humanity without as much comedy.

"Tenzin and I," Ben started, "have been heading up a new branch of Giovanni's business."

"I've heard a bit," Max said. "New York, right? Working in O'Brien territory?"

"We have an agreement with them, yes." He took a drink. "Unlike Giovanni's branch, Tenzin and I have cast a wider net. We're less focused."

"And by that you mean...?"

"We find things for people who are missing them. Not

people. We're not casting the net that wide. But if it's a thing that can be found, we can find it."

Were his claims grandstanding and dubious optimism? Yes. Ben went with it anyway. No one got anywhere by being overly modest.

Max said, "And I'm assuming you have some experience in this?"

"Tenzin and I have been working together for about three years. Mostly word of mouth. You may have heard about our recovery of Sicilian tarí in Naples last summer."

"Oh!" Cathy said. "I do remember hearing about that. It was right around the time the Mad Duke bit it, right?"

"Yes," Tenzin said. "We were there for that."

"Exciting." Cathy's eyes lit up.

"I thought so. Ben, not as much."

There was so much he could say... but Ben bit his tongue. He sensed that Cathy and Tenzin had similar ideas of "fun."

Max shrugged. "I can't lie, Ben, this all seems very interesting. But I don't sense you need an investor, and I'm not in the market for any lost items. What do you want from me?"

"I want you to hire us," Ben said.

Cathy laughed. "He takes after his uncle."

Max laughed. "Whatever for?"

"We have information on an object that we believe might be highly prized by you and your family," Ben said.

"Oh?" Max said. "And what would that be?"

"The Sanguine Raptor." Ben took a drink and observed Max and Cathy's faces. Max's face was carefully blank. Cathy's was alight with excitement.

"Max, is that the sword—?"

"Yes." He cut her off with one word and an expression Cathy was quick enough to read.

48

"Oh," Cathy said. "That's interesting." Then she took a long swallow of her cider.

Ben waited. Then he waited some more.

Silence did not sit comfortably at the table.

"The Sanguine Raptor is... lost," Max said. "Arcane. Despite some local wives' tales, it passed into legend centuries ago."

"And yet..." Ben wanted to speak carefully. He had no idea if René had come north. No idea if Gemma shared his meeting with Tywyll. "There has never been any proof that it was destroyed or stolen. In fact, *none* of Brennus's treasure was ever found."

Max smiled. "Don't you think it would have been if it existed?"

Ben shrugged. "I don't know. The Staffordshire hoard was found intact by a retiree with a metal detector. Anything is possible."

Max examined him, and Ben tried to regulate his breathing. His pulse. Any tell that might give Max more information than he wanted to share.

"So..." Max steepled his fingers with his elbows on the table. "You really think you can find Brennus's treasure?"

"I wouldn't be here if I didn't."

"You've some... clue that leads to gold missing for twelve hundred years?"

Ben said, "I don't want to get too specific, but... yes."

"If that's true, what do you need me for?"

"I told you. I want you to hire us."

Max leaned forward. "To fund you?"

"No. Just to hire us. We can negotiate a split for the treasure."

The corner of Max's mouth turned up in a rueful smile. "You're audacious, I'll give you that."

"This isn't about the money."

Max's smile turned patronizing. "Young man, *everything* in our world is about money."

"In my opinion, it's more about currency. And money is only one kind of currency." Ben set down his drink. "Tell you what, do you have a five-pound note on you?"

Amused, Max pulled a slim wallet from the inner pocket of his jacket. He pulled out a five-pound note and set it in Ben's hand.

"There," Ben said. "I'm hired."

"That's all you want? Five pounds?"

"No, I want more than that," Ben said. "I want permission to search in this territory. Not only are you of Brennus's line, you're connected. If you and Cathy give your permission, the vampire in charge of this territory won't cause any problems for me."

Cathy said, "That's true."

"And you're certain Brennus's treasure is within this territory?"

Ben continued as if he hadn't heard Max's question. "I don't want to keep the majority of the gold for myself. I'll split it with you, and I think you'd find the split more than equitable."

"Why are you doing this?" Max asked. "The money?"

"I told you, it's not about the money."

"Then why?" Max cocked his head. "The sword?"

Ben smiled but didn't say another word.

"Do you truly think it's real?" Max asked.

"I know it is."

"You're not the first who has looked for it, you know."

"Brennus's treasure—and the Sanguine Raptor—are legends," Ben said. "I want to be a legend too."

Max smiled. "Now that is a motivation I can appreciate." He pulled out a hundred-pound note. "There. Add that to the five and you're officially hired. Ben Vecchio, I want you to find my great-grandsire's treasure or die trying."

Tenzin reached out and swiped the hundred-pound note. "He's not taking a death oath."

"Relax, Tenzin," Ben said. "I'm pretty sure Max is joking."

Tenzin's eyes fixed on Max. "Maybe. Maybe not. But words have power, Benjamin. And I'll take that oath before you do."

"Tenzin, you're not taking a death oath either."

"Exactly."

"Fine," Max said. "Benjamin Vecchio, I want you to find"—Max couldn't stop an amused smile—"the treasure hoard of my great-grandsire and bring it to me. If you don't succeed, you'll owe me twice again what I've paid you for this task."

"Those are terms you can agree to," Tenzin said. She held on to the note.

"Thanks so much." Ben held out his hand and Max shook it. "Looking forward to this."

Cathy clapped and a spark shot from between her hands. "And I thought this winter was going to be boring."

4

I T WAS AMAZING HOW EARLY the sun set in Edinburgh in the fall. By four o'clock in the afternoon, it looked like nighttime in California. Streetlights went on and golden light rippled on the damp black stones that made up the Royal Mile.

While the setting sun meant little for most humans who tromped up and down the road between Holyrood and Edinburgh Castle—some tourists, some festivalgoers, some everyday citizens of the old city—the setting sun had always meant something different to Ben.

Here there be monsters.

As a child, night was the time his mother let her demons out to play, falling into the sad oblivion of the bottle. Sometimes his father would come in the dark, shouting and throwing money at her, tossing dire threats before he stormed off, forgetting about the skinny boy until it came time for the next round of money and recrimination. Junkies woke at night, their greedy, distant eyes searching to see if a little boy had anything worth taking.

Ben had learned to hide before he could read.

Other predators roamed too. They were the ones who made Ben's skin crawl. Their eyes weren't distant, and the greed was of a different kind. When Ben's instincts told him to run, he ran.

Now the monsters came in the form of friends and adversaries, immortal creatures who seduced with pale and beautiful faces. Tricksters who seemed more genteel than human predators... until you looked into cold eyes that saw you as food.

For Ben Vecchio, the night had always been owned by monsters.

He moved up Lawnmarket to the flat he'd leased in James Court. He'd rented it months before, anticipating a long-term stay in the city. With so many tourists around, Ben could be just another face in the crowd, but the flat itself was in one of the massive stone buildings surrounding an open courtyard. It was thick-walled and nearly light-proof. Once he'd ducked off the Royal Mile, Ben was concealed from most prying eyes. Tenzin was able to come and go at night, taking advantage of the black courtyards, narrow alleyways, and steep side streets that curved like ribs branching from the spine of old Edinburgh.

"Not that we'll be here much longer." His murmured words frosted the night air as he hummed a tune playing from one of the many pubs he passed. He didn't know where Tenzin was, but he was nearly certain that she'd be back at the flat unless she'd decided to disappear on him like she had the night before.

"Mr. Vecchio, isn't it?"

Ben paused when someone called his name. He turned, looking over his shoulder.

Well, hell.

"What a wonderful coincidence to meet you here."

René Dupont leaned against the wall of Deacon Brodie's Tavern, two tourists, a man and a woman, hanging off his arms.

"René Dupont," Ben said. "What a surprise."

"Hello, my friend." René glanced up and down the still-busy street. "I see you are also here to delight in the sounds of the Scottish Fiddle Festival."

"Oh yeah," Ben said. "Every year. Never miss it."

René smirked. "So I thought."

Ben nodded toward the two humans, who were clearly under the influence of René's amnis. The couple looked like typical tourists, stuffed backpacks and crisp coats. One even had a camera hanging around her neck.

"New friends?" he asked.

René ran a finger along the woman's cheek. She smiled and sighed, leaning into his touch. "They asked me if I was interested in showing them 'another side of the city' when we were chatting at the bar. I decided to take them up on it." He lifted an eyebrow. "I don't think they were talking about a local tour."

Ben examined the couple, uncertain how to proceed. Mostly likely René would feed from the humans and be on his way. Sex might or might not happen. Every vampire was different, and some had no morals about seducing humans with amnis.

"Relax, honorable young Vecchio," René said. "I know who the enforcer is in this town. Cathy has burned me before, and I'm fairly sure she enjoyed it. Feeding guidelines are strict in this city no matter how willing the participants may be."

"They're under the influence."

René shrugged. "They were well on their way before they met me."

Cathy was a fire vampire, and it wasn't a secret that William, Lord MacGregor, the vampire in charge of Edinburgh, kept her around because of her ferocity. Edinburgh was a city that owed much to its reputation as a safe city for tourists, festival attendees, and students. MacGregor couldn't have any of them reporting assaults or strange attacks at night. Cathy made sure it didn't happen.

"What are you doing in Edinburgh, René?"

"I am visiting my uncle, of course." René smiled. "I love Max. Such a wonderful chef, if you get a chance to taste his cooking. Excellent taste in whisky. But what are *you* doing here?"

"Taking in the sights, of course."

"I do hope your alluring associate is with you." René glanced up and down the street again. Then overhead. "Should I be so lucky, my friend?"

"No," Ben said flatly. "I am pretty sure you'll never be that lucky."

"Oh, my dear human, has she rebuffed you?" René cocked his head. "Do not despair. It is likely your mortal body has little to tempt her other than blood. It is only natural."

Ben ignored him. Typical vampire superiority. "Why are you here, René?"

"There is a charming exhibit at the National Museum I was hoping to see. Jade ax-heads from the Italian Alps." He shivered. "I'm passionate about the Stone Age."

"Really?"

"I am only sorry I missed the Celts exhibit earlier this year. Did you happen to see it?" René's eyes gleamed.

"I did. Too bad you missed it. But then, you should probably get used to missing things."

René laughed. "You are so confident. In a way, it is endearing."

"Yeah, I hear that all the time." Ben clenched his hands in his pockets. "I'm super-endearing. Adorable even."

"I have no doubt." René shrugged off the arms of the tourist couple and stepped toward Ben. His voice dropped, and all pretense of amusement fell. "You are mistaken, my friend, if you think my interest in the Sanguine Raptor is frivolous or passing. I know you believe you know the location of Brennus's sword. My intention is to find it before you. And if that fails, I will simply take it from you."

Ben smiled. "Do you think so?"

"I know it." René stepped within inches of Ben. He reached up, but Ben grabbed his wrist before he could make contact, yanking René's hand away from his face and forcing his wrist back.

"Not a good idea." No vampire would be making contact with Ben's bare skin unless he knew they were a friend. He'd learned his lesson on that one.

"You are quite strong for a human, aren't you?" René's eyes lit with mischief. "What can I say? I am so curious what all the fuss is about."

"It's good to wonder about things," Ben said, stepping back and releasing René's wrist. "Have a good night."

"Say hello to Tenzin for me."

"No."

"She'll smell me on your skin," René said. "I shall savor the thought until I see her again."

BEN SMELLED the cardamom and ginger when he walked in the door. "Tiny, you read my mind."

"Not lately," Tenzin called from the kitchen.

Ben blinked. "Wait... what?"

"How was New Town? Did it take long to walk?"

Ben hung his coat and kicked off his boots before he headed to the kitchen. "Have you been using amnis on me?"

"Of course not." She slid from the stove to the sink in her stocking feet. "How was New Town? Did you find what you were looking for?"

"Yes." He walked over and spun Tenzin around, pushing her against the counter and trapping her between his arms. "Have you been using amnis on me?"

Her eyes went wide. "No."

His temper, held in careful check during his meeting with Dupont, spiked. "Dammit, Tenzin. You know that's not allowed. We talked about that when you asked to stay at the loft."

"You were talking in your sleep again." She patted his cheek. "I just put you back to sleep. Don't overreact."

He stepped away. Ben didn't want to know what he said in his sleep. At times like this, ignorance was bliss.

"Don't do it again." He reached over her shoulder and stuck a finger in the curry. "Hot!"

She slapped his hand. "Don't do that."

He sucked off the sauce that tasted something close to a spicy korma. "That's good. Lamb?"

"Yes."

"Where'd you get lamb?"

She went still.

He closed his eyes. "Tenzin, if you're snatching random sheep from some farmer, I need to know about it. And... I don't even want to think about where you may have cleaned—"

"Ha!" She grinned. "I got you. Max gave me the name of the late-night butcher he and Cathy use."

Oh thank God. Ben was trying to imagine scrubbing frozen sheep guts off the stones in the courtyard before the neighbors woke up.

"I'm glad you're finally getting the hang of this using money to buy food thing." He reached over her head and grabbed bowls and plates from the cupboard. The flat had come fully furnished, but the furnishings were sparse. Since it was just the two of them, it wasn't a problem. He hoped they wouldn't have company though.

"Speaking of company," he started.

"Were we speaking of company?" She leaned over and sniffed his jacket. "You saw the Frenchman."

"Caught that?"

She wrinkled her nose. "There's a cologne he uses. It's distinctive."

Ben sniffed his shirt. "I didn't smell anything."

"You wouldn't." She stirred the simmering pot. "So our friend René is in Edinburgh, is he?"

"He was disappointed not to see you." He set the plates out, put the bowls next to the stove, and opened the drawer for the silverware. He grabbed a spoon for Tenzin, which was the only kind of flatware she liked. "He knows we're here after the Sanguine Raptor."

"Gemma did warn us about that."

"I'm debating whether or not to call Max. René said he was visiting his uncle, but that may have been a lie."

She shrugged. "He's your client. This one is up to you."

That was the problem. Ben was still figuring out how to properly plan and run a job of this scale. He was sure he was capable of it... most of the time. But the majority of his past experience had been scrambling after Tenzin, cleaning up her messes. Planning and executing a job of this size took an entirely different perspective.

It was also a new way of operating for Tenzin, who had taken jobs in the past, but mostly for mercenary work. Hunting immortals required a slightly different skill set than hunting artifacts.

"Wine or beer?" he asked.

"Beer, but nothing dark."

"Got it." He pulled two bottles of bitter out of the cooler. "So, the Register House was good. I think I've narrowed it down enough to go for a drive tomorrow."

She heaped his bowl with a mound of fragrant rice, then spooned the lamb overtop before she served herself a smaller portion. "A drive to...?"

"I'll tell you in the morning," he said. "Right now we should enjoy this food, because I am starving."

"You're always starving."

"And you always feed me." He leaned over and kissed the top of her head. "No wonder we make such great partners."

St. Andrews, Scotland

THE WOMAN WAS TWENTY-FIVE, but her green eyes looked older. She was tall and leggy in a way that reminded Ben that the Vikings really got around back in the day. Her pale face was pretty and freckled. Blond hair whipped across her face from the sea breeze as she crossed the narrow street to the cafe, ducking in just before the rain came down. She paused at the door, looking for him. Ben looked up from the phone held in his hand, nodding at her over his steaming cup of coffee. Just another random student staring at his mobile phone and reading his Twitter feed in the bustling university town of Saint Andrews.

She spotted him and walked over, a set of keys clutched in her hand.

Excellent.

Ben looked around, but no one noticed the girl. The people she passed barely looked up.

People were so easy to distract now; all they did was look at their phones. Ben figured the only person who'd looked him in the face since he walked in the door was the woman who took his order at the counter.

Annoying? A little. But it made it much harder for a vampire looking for him to question humans later.

Thanks, technology.

The girl was named Susan. She was a student at the university and the sister of one of Max's day-people. She sat down in the chair across from him and tried to tuck her hair back into a bun. She wasn't too successful.

"Can I get you a coffee?" Ben asked.

"No thanks."

Ben had taken the train up the coast and stayed at a hotel in the town center after taking a cab into town. Classes were still in session, so the streets were busy and businesses were full. He'd made no secret of his presence in the city—if anyone was looking for him, they could find him—but he'd been wary about renting a car. He didn't mind people—okay, René—knowing he was in Saint Andrews, but he didn't want anyone to know what kind of car he was driving.

That was were Susan came in.

"The car is not mine. It's my neighbor's, and I sang her a story about my desperate and pitiful young American friend." Susan kept her hands and the keys folded on her lap. "So if you're trouble and don't bring the car back, Max and Cathy will know. The money you're paying me isn't going to cover the cost of a new car, even if it is just a Corsa."

He smiled. "You're telling me you haven't already called them?"

"Maybe."

"If you didn't, you're not as smart as I thought you were."

"Jarod asked Max. He vouched for you."

"What else did he ask?"

Susan rolled her eyes. "Do you think we're new? The less I know, the better. I don't even want to know your name. I want my money and for you to return the car by next week." Her eyes narrowed. "You're not a shitty American driver, are you?"

"Of course I'm not a shitty American driver." He reached his hand out, and she put the keys in it. "Kind of a shit British driver though. Whole thing about the wheel being on the wrong side of the car, you know?"

Susan stood. "Don't be an arse. Just because you know important people doesn't mean your blood doesn't run as easily as any other human's."

He held out an envelope that she grabbed and stuffed in her messenger bag. "All you need to do is keep quiet and pretend you never saw me," he said. "The car will be back in its parking spot in a week. And tell your friend thanks. Just don't use my name."

"Handy." She wrapped her scarf more tightly around her neck and raised her hood. "As I don't know your name. Don't crash the car, nameless American."

Ben couldn't help but like her. "Is this that rumored Highland hospitality?"

She curled her lip. "Does it look like we're in the Highlands to you?"

Without another word, she turned and walked out the door. The wind was so strong it took some leaning to push it open. Then Susan was out the door, and Ben had a car.

And coffee.

Glancing at the downpour happening outside, he decided he had enough time to finish the coffee.

FIVE DAYS LATER, he'd secured a completely different vehicle, an empty vacation cottage nearer the probable site, and all the supplies he'd need for a prolonged hunt. Nothing was under his name. Most of the reservations had been made over the phone. Supplies had been ordered online and delivered to the house. There was a small barn at the rear of the cottage that would work for storing the car. Ben would be working on foot, and he'd be working during the day.

He didn't care what Tenzin thought. Daylight searching was imperative.

He took the train back to Edinburgh after leaving the car parked where he'd promised Susan. The old Jeep had been stored at the cottage. He'd be able to take a cab or walk from the Leuchars train station depending on the weather.

By his estimation, the search for Brennus's gold should take three days in the field. He hadn't seen a hint of René Dupont anywhere around Saint Andrews, but that meant little. Ben had been making an effort to show up at the normal tourist sites in town and making himself known as a regular at a number of markets and cafes. If René was following him, Ben wanted to be the one placing the bread crumbs.

The announcer's voice woke him to the approaching station. "Next station, Haymarket."

Ben roused himself from a light nap and realized he'd be getting into the city just after dark. He knew Tenzin barely slept. What was René's habit? Most older vampires didn't need a full twelve hours of sleep a day, but most did sleep. This time of year, vampires had fifteen full hours of darkness to play with. Ben had only nine hours of light.

Why had he planned this trip for the winter? The lack of tourists and the busyness of the university town suddenly seemed to pale in comparison to the luxurious hours of daylight—and dry weather—he would have had available during a Scottish summer.

Of course, it also meant he had Tenzin as a resource with longer nights. And since Tenzin did *not* sleep, winter meant a happier and less housebound partner.

He gathered his backpack and exited the train at Waverley station. A crowd of evening commuters barely let him pass by before they crowded on the train heading north out of the city and toward Dundee. Unsurprisingly, it was raining. He lifted the hood on his jacket, tucked his phone in the inside pocket, and walked up the hill and toward the flat where he hoped some food would mysteriously appear.

Up the steps and up the hill. Dodging loitering tourists, brisk businessmen, and the ever present pipers on the Royal Mile, he trudged up the damp street toward the dark shelter of the north passage to James Court. He ducked in and entered the code for the doorway, pulling open the heavy door and letting it close behind him.

Ben let out a breath. Silence.

The cold stone walls blocked out the bustle of people and automobiles, pipers and vendors.

As he walked up the old spiral stairs, he heard a sound he hadn't been expecting.

Laughter.

Male laughter.

The laughter went silent as he approached the door. Quiet shuffling. His key went in the lock.

Ben walked in with his hand on his knife. When he saw who Tenzin was entertaining, he felt no urge to remove his hand, but he did have to restrain himself from pulling the blade.

Tenzin had been cooking again. But this time her guest was René Dupont.

5

_____

W ELL, THIS SHOULD BE INTERESTING.
Tenzin set down her spoon and wondered just
how wise her Benjamin had grown.

"You're back!" she said brightly.

"I am." His face was... not so bright.

But that was fine. He needed to scratch a bit of the
brightness off if he wanted to survive in the immortal world.

"René found our flat," she said.

"I can see that."

"I invited him for dinner."

Ben set his messenger bag down on the armchair and
leaned his shoulder against the large stone chimney on the
opposite side of the room. "You invited him for dinner," he
said. "Were you that hard up to find fresh blood?"

René's mouth turned up at the corner. "Witty."

"Curious," Ben said.

"I am no vampire's meal."

"Bet you wish you were," Ben said. "Why are you in
my flat?"

"I understood I was invited."

"Not by me."

Tenzin tried not to roll her eyes at the posturing. They were both so young. They were like two roosters puffing out their chests. Obviously she needed to intervene before the spurs came out. "I invited René to our flat when I found him feeding—very indiscreetly, I might add—in the pub where we heard the loud music."

Ben said, "That could literally be any pub in the surrounding area. You have told me nothing."

"I invited him here"—she ignored his boring disapproval and continued—"so we could have an honest discussion about the Sanguine Raptor."

René looked disappointed, though his smile hid it well. Ben looked quietly outraged.

"Why?" Ben asked.

"Because he wants it." Tenzin stepped between Ben and René. "Look at him," she said to Ben. "He's clearly not a swordsman. Watch the way he moves; he has no sense of balance. He'd be pathetic with a blade."

René stood and began cursing at her in quiet French, but Tenzin put a hand on his chest and shoved him back in the chair.

"So he doesn't want the blade for himself," she continued. "He wants it as treasure. You heard him speaking with Gemma. He's not sentimental, even with his immortal clan. Which means he has a buyer for the treasure. Which means we should find out who they are and see if we can make a deal with them." She glanced over her shoulder. "I mean, I'm fairly sure I know who it is already, but I wanted to confirm."

René curled his lip. "I changed my mind. I don't find you charming at all."

"Yes, you do." Tenzin smiled. "You don't want to, but you do. It's the power."

His silent glare said everything Tenzin wanted.

She knew there were always some vampires, both male and female, who were drawn to her because of her age and elemental strength. It was like a magnet. For some, the attraction was pure instinct. For others, it was calculation. Either way, it taught her to be circumspect.

She turned back to Ben. "If you want me to kick him out, I can. But I made enough for three, so it's up to you."

"No." René stood and smoothed the front of his jacket. "It is up to *me*. You disappoint me, Tenzin."

"You wound me, René."

A smile forced itself to his lips, and Tenzin changed her opinion of him in an instant. René was more complicated than she'd initially judged. He *was* attracted to her, but it wasn't calculation. Or not entirely. Despite her suspicions, she liked him a little.

"I see your game," he said quietly. "I decide not to play it."

"Come now." Tenzin walked over and flicked a minuscule piece of lint off his shoulder. "You were playing a game too."

"I suspected you would be a horrible liar," René said. "And you are."

"I know," Tenzin said, making her eyes as wide as possible. "Which is why you should probably practice with a blade more. You favor your left side."

"You think?" The Frenchman wrapped his cashmere scarf around his neck and shrugged on his coat. "*Au revoir, ma petite,*" he said. "We will meet again." He glanced at Ben. "Tell your human his clumsy attempts to mislead me were not successful."

"I'll be sure to do that," she said. "Good-bye."

Without a backward glance, he walked to the door and left the flat. Tenzin waited until the heavy metal door to the passageway swung shut.

"Well, at least he's not one of those villains who always has to have the last word," Tenzin said. "Those are so annoying."

"Did you find out what you wanted?" Ben slid his hunting knife back in its sheath and walked to the counter. "And did you *really* need to invite him into our flat?"

She sprawled on the couch. "It seemed like the thing to do at the time."

"I'm making tea. It's freezing out there. Do you want some?"

"Please."

Ben filled the kettle and set it on the stove before he turned around and leaned his hip against the counter. She could see the smile flirting at the corner of his mouth. "So you're a bad liar, huh?"

"Pathetic. Didn't you know that?"

"Ha!" Ben shook his head and let the smile break through. "Did you find what you wanted?"

"No, but I will. He'll contact whoever hired him, and I'll figure out who it is." Tenzin floated from the couch and over to the windows. She glanced outside before she closed the heavy wooden shutters. They blocked out the lovely twinkling lights from the streetlamps and signs, but they helped keep the flat warm too. Buildings of this age were chilly in the best weather. In the damp cold, they could be miserable.

"And his threat about following me?" Ben asked.

"Empty. I was tracking him since nightfall. He hasn't

left the city and he can't fly. The most he got was that you took a train to Saint Andrews."

Ben smiled. "Good."

"Are you set up wherever you need to be?"

He nodded. "You staying around here for a couple of days?"

"I want to watch the Frenchman for a few more nights. He reacted too perfectly. I'm either getting more psychic, he's really that predictable, or there's something we're not seeing. He's not dumb. He's smart, and he's played this game longer than we have. We shouldn't underestimate him."

The kettle whistled and Ben filled the teapot. "Fine. I'll be working during the day anyway. You won't be able to help. Might as well stay around here and see what he's up to."

She smiled. "And that's all you're giving me about your brilliant plan?"

"Hey, turnabout's fair play." He winked at her and grabbed two mugs for tea. "It's not like you've been Miss Let's Share All the Details in the past."

"Does this mean I'm going to get trapped on a submarine crossing the ocean back to New York?"

"If everything goes according to plan? Yes."

"Good to know you've worked through your issues on that," she said in Chinese.

He answered in kind, setting a pot of tea on the table. "Be quiet and drink your tea, you wide-eyed innocent."

"THIS?" Two nights later, she was staring at... She didn't know what it was, exactly. All she knew was that it made the most alarming noise when she approached it. "What is this? This is your brilliant plan?"

Ben tromped into the cottage, mud up to his knees, bundled in plaid, and clearly in a foul mood. "Did I ask you? Give me a minute to get warm before you start interrogating me."

"What is it?"

He hung the contraption on a hook by the garden door as he sat and tried to remove his mud-encrusted rubber boots. "That is the Garrett ATX metal detector," he said, yanking off one boot. "Waterproof. Thirteen different sensitivity levels. Seven hundred thirty pulses per second."

Tenzin's mouth dropped open. "You're using a... a metal detector? To search for one of the largest caches of gold in immortal history?"

"The size of the cache is only rumors." He yanked off the second boot. "And yes. I'm using a metal detector. It worked in Staffordshire."

"That was an exception, not a winning business breakthrough."

He leaned against the wall, and Tenzin could see how tired he was. "Tiny, I'm exhausted. I'm not getting into this with you tonight. What did you expect me to do? Hire a friendly neighborhood earth vampire to walk the grid with me?"

"Yes, because that is an excellent idea. Unlike a metal detector, which is not."

He straightened and stretched his shoulders back. "No."

"Why not?"

Ben said, "First, I'd have to work at night, making me more conspicuous to vampires. Second, I'd have to tell someone else the treasure is here—"

"*Probably* here."

"Definitely here." The first smile broke through his exhaustion. "Go look in the bread box, Tiny."

Tenzin walked over to the small kitchen and opened the wooden box where she smelled stale bread.

"See the teacup in there with all the loose American change?"

She found the teacup. "And?"

"Shake it out. You expect me to do all the work for you?"" He rose to his feet and stretched. His sweater rode up, exposing the pale line of his stomach and the dark line of hair on his abdomen.

He really was becoming annoyingly tall. Tenzin looked away and back to the coins in the cup. She poured them into her hand and felt the moment it touched.

Gold.

She smiled and put the other money back, letting the single gold coin settle in the palm of her hand.

There was nothing like the energy gold emitted. Some would call her superstitious, but they weren't as old as she was. They hadn't seen the eternal metal as she had. Hadn't felt it surrounding them.

The paltry treasure hoards of the modern age were nothing in comparison to those of kings and empresses of the past. Tenzin had walked in rooms layered in gold, had drunk blood from solid hammered goblets, had eaten food sprinkled with its dust.

She'd taken a king for a lover who painted her body with gold dust just to see her outline on silk sheets after they'd made love.

The weight of the small coin made her smile. To the less-experienced eye, it would appear Macedonian. It wasn't. It was early Gallic, and in excellent condition.

She asked, "Where did you find it?"

"Near the bank where the stream branches." Ben took a towel and rubbed at his hair, which had grown damp with the evening mist. "I decided to keep going with my grid for the time being, but I'm focusing on the search areas closest to the stream. If the geological surveys are correct, there's a limited area where any cache of significance could be buried."

"Unless it's in a cave formed by an immortal," Tenzin said. "Those don't show up on geological surveys."

"Tenzin, I'm not calling an earth vampire to help us look."

"Why not?"

"It's just one more person knowing that we're looking in this location." He draped the towel across his shoulders. "And the last thing we need is someone blabbing—"

"I could probably..." She paused. Ben would most likely *not* approve of looking for a rival vampire and using them to search before dispatching them.

He frowned. "You could probably what?"

"Nothing." She glanced at the nonsentient machine he'd been using. "Your machine sounds very interesting. Tell me more about it."

His eyes narrowed. "No."

"What?" She made her eyes very big again. It had worked well with the Frenchman. "You don't want me to know about the machine?"

"You know that's not what I'm talking about." The eye trick did not work with Ben. He rose and walked toward her. "Whatever you were thinking just now. No."

"I don't know what you're talking about."

"I'm sure you don't." He grabbed a can of beer from the cooler and cracked it open. "Isn't my metal detector nice?"

"Yes, very nice." She smiled, but he did not look reassured. "And, of course, vampires wouldn't be able to use something like that. Excellent planning, Benjamin."

SHE RESTED THAT DAY, meditating and watching over Ben as he slept. But the next night, she flew over the search area while Ben was making notes on his grid. She was glad he'd spent a few days turning up nothing. He was learning one of the cardinal rules of treasure hunting: Most of it was boring. Patience was rewarded; daring was not. Tenzin had the patience of a hunting cat. When she was focused on something, she could wait as long as necessary for her prey to reveal itself. And riches were her favorite kind of prey.

The countryside was deserted and high fog rolled in off the North Sea. She flew over the trees and ducked between them to land in the wooded glade of Dunino Den. She breathed deeply; the ancient energy of the wood surrounded her, and she understood immediately why Ben had been so certain of this location. The air felt heavy, and the wind spoke to her, removed from the roar of modern life and humanity. This was an old place.

Trees, brush, and exposed rock marked the tiny corner of wild. Moss hung heavy from trees and lichen decorated rocks. The stream had swollen with the recent rain, and the sound of rushing water filled the air along with the scent of moldering debris. She walked up the den, letting her fingers flutter over the ribbons and beads tied among the bushes. Wilted flowers, leaves, and lovers' tokens hung on an ancient stump at the center of the glade.

"Humble folk still be hanging ribbons at the Raven King's tree."

How had Tywyll known Ben was thinking of this place?

She passed the old stump and walked beside the exposed limestone that bordered the natural amphitheater. Her fingers traced the crosses and symbols inscribed on the rock and she floated up to investigate. Some artist had added the visage of a gnarled face with a wide nose and full beard. The scowling face emerged from the rock, a silent and disapproving witness to the pilgrims who offered their gifts. She floated up the stone steps cutting through the twin outcroppings and let the night wind speak to her.

"Ravens like ribbons, but they like silver more."

She reached the top of the steps and saw the pool in front of her. It was a round ceremonial well. The holy men who came later would have taken it for their own purposes, but Tenzin spotted the hollowed-out footprint at its edge. To the immortal eye, it was clear evidence of an earth vampire.

Brennus?

But Ben had said this was a Pictish site.

"...he didn't have a coin for the new king's stone."

That phrase was the key. Those were the words that had made Ben's eyes come alive. Tenzin had heard *king's* but had Tywyll been saying *kings*? Who were the new kings? Would the Picts have been the "new kings" to an ancient like Brennus?

The new kings' stone...

Tenzin wandered up the path with the wind whispering in her ears.

The new king's stone.

The new kings' stone.

She walked the narrow lane between the woods and the churchyard, drawn to the graves that dotted the deep green grass. She passed an old headstone with the penitent's face worn away by time. A mourner was carved into the edge of the granite, her hood smooth and worn by water and wind. Past the headstone in the moonlight, Tenzin caught the shine of silver.

"...he didn't have a coin for the new kings' stone."

She stepped closer and bent to inspect the coins, careful not to move any of them. Currency from all over was piled on top of the lichen- and moss-covered rock. Silver and nickel mostly. Some copper. Some brass. It wasn't a gravestone, it was a standing stone or the stump of one. The ground was cleared around the stone, as if someone had cut back the grass around the base.

What was this place? A holy tree. A ceremonial well. A standing stone.

A place of ritual. Of spiritual power. A natural amphitheater.

Dunino Den was a place of holiness, ritual, and authority.

Her eyes fell to the standing stone covered in coins. In offerings.

In... tribute.

"You should always bring a coin for the Raven King's throne."

Tenzin went to her knees before the old stone and scraped back more of the grass to bare the soil. She sank her hands into the packed dirt and bent, putting her mouth to the ground. She held back the instinctive revulsion at the taste of earth against her lips so she could concentrate on breathing out the air that would speak to her. She exhaled, forcing her amnis into the ground with her element.

Then she closed her eyes and waited. Her hair hung around her like a curtain, brushing the grass and gathering water as she waited.

She waited.

Her breath crawled along roots and under rocks, seeking tiny spaces to possess. It traveled along grains of rock and rotting vegetation. It traveled down.

Down.

Down.

Tenzin sank into her mind. Dug her fingers into the ground and let the air within her connect to the night and the blackness and the space in all things. She felt the night birds move over her and the wind moving the trees. She dissolved into her senses and the amnis within all things.

She waited.

Until the air she'd breathed from her body found the hidden places she'd been seeking. It crawled and explored, tasted and gathered secrets. Then the air came back to her, whispering tales of gods and treasures.

The new kings' stone.

The Raven King's throne.

Tenzin started awake from her trance, tasting the soil on her lips. She sat up and put a hand on the strange rock, her eyes wide and her mind racing.

"Brennus," she whispered. "You clever bastard."

6

BEN WOKE THAT AFTERNOON, HIS body rolling into the beam of light that cut across the bed in the west bedroom. He could hear Tenzin in the front part of the house, moving with her familiar lightness, a fluid combination of walking and flying that marked her presence to his ears. He lay in the angled light and let the sun warm his face.

It was no coincidence that he'd chosen this room for his bedchamber, just as it was no coincidence that he slept better in the day. Sun meant safety. For the past week, he'd been working days, searching the glade and streambed, and he'd been restless at night until Tenzin had arrived. His sleep had completely turned around, and it felt good to enjoy a long nap in the afternoon sun.

He heard the kettle whistle and knew Tenzin had put the tea on, which meant she knew he was awake. He enjoyed one last stretch in the sunbeam, a scratch on his belly, and then he rose, unfolding his limbs from the short bed in the cottage. He threw on a flannel shirt and made his way out to the kitchen, forcing his hair into submission under a knitted beanie as he debated for the hundredth time whether or not he should shave it all off.

"Good evening," Tenzin said. "Or afternoon, I suppose."

"You went exploring last night." He slumped at the kitchen table, still not quite awake, and rubbed his eyes. "When did you get back?"

"Six or seven?" She filled the teapot and Ben enjoyed the rising aroma of bergamot and black tea. "You were in your room scribbling, so I decided not to interrupt you. Then I think you fell asleep."

"I haven't been sleeping at night," he said with a yawn. "And I've been working during the day, so yeah. A bit exhausted."

She turned toward him, and for a moment, her eyes were so sharp with pain his breath caught in his chest.

"Tenzin?"

The moment dissipated like steam in a cold room. "I do miss sleep. Sometimes I miss sleep."

Tenzin wasn't one to complain about... well, anything. Not seriously. She only whined to annoy him or tease.

"I didn't know you missed it," he said carefully. "You don't get tired though, do you?"

"It's not physical. I meditate to rest," she said, turning back to the cupboard and getting two mugs for tea. "But I don't get tired. Not like humans do. Not in my body. Just my mind."

"I think anyone would. I'm glad meditation helps."

"But sometimes..." Her eyes drifted again. "Sometimes you need more. You need a break. Most of the past century was a break for me. I went into the mountains with Nima and I just... was. I didn't see anyone. I didn't talk to anyone."

Ben remained frozen. It was so unusual for Tenzin to

speak about her past, he feared the slightest movement would break whatever strange spell was causing her to confide in him.

"Giovanni had left me," she continued. "He'd become tired of mercenary work. I was too. The human world became violent on a different scale. Wars were global. Everything was changing so fast. I decided to take a break."

"In Tibet. With Nima."

"Yes. Most of us do, you know."

"Take a break?"

"Yes. Very old vampires become tired or bored or over-whelmed. We debate going into the sun. Some of us do." Her eyes met his. "But then others who are still hungry for life... we sleep. Not as humans do. It's a kind of stasis. In my longest stasis, I became a living idol. My cave became a shrine, and I fed from those who came to pray to me."

"No one tried to harm you?"

She shook her head, and her eyes became less dreamy. Sharper. "The humans thought I was a goddess. Because to them, I had always been there. Never moving. Never aging. But I wasn't asleep. If something had tried to attack me, I would have protected myself."

"But nothing did."

Tenzin poured the tea and added a twist of lemon to hers and milk to his. She walked over and sat at the kitchen table across from him. "No, nothing did. They left treasure for me. Beautiful things. Many of them are still in that cave."

Ben tried not to salivate at the thought of a hidden trea-sure cave in the Himalayas. "The humans didn't take the treasure?"

"Of course not. They were offerings," Tenzin said,

leaning closer. "Offerings to a god. To take them would have been... unwise."

...he didn't have a coin for the new king's stone...

Ben sipped his tea. Put the mug down. Thought about their strange conversation and the growing knot in his gut. "You're not just feeling chatty, are you?"

Tenzin shook her head.

His conversation with Tywyll leapt to his memory. *"Brennus didn't give me permission to share where he buried the* Fitheach Lann, *so I suppose we're at an impasse..."*

Past tense. Or so he'd thought. "Tiny, if you're saying—"

"Brennus is alive," she said. "He was never killed. You found his treasure, but you found the Raven King too."

BEN SAT with his notes and charts and maps spread in front of him. Pictures and drawings. Old survey maps and handwritten accounts. Small mountains of paperwork and notes. Over a year's worth of research.

Tenzin sat across from him. "You have to leave it."

But he couldn't. He'd done too much work. He had a client. His *first* client. A client who had hired him to find the Sanguine Raptor, the *Fitheach Lann*, or whatever old vampires wanted to call it. And now he had René Dupont in Edinburgh. He didn't have time to restrategize.

And it was just one sword...

He could leave the treasure if Brennus was still alive. All he needed was one sword and his reputation would be established. He'd be twenty-four and his reputation in the immortal world and the antiquities collecting market would be set.

He pulled at the hair that had escaped from his hat. "One sword, Tenzin."

"Stop it," Tenzin said. "You don't know what you're asking for if you try to unearth him."

"Weren't you the one who got more excited at the idea of stealing from a living vampire than a dead one?"

"That was when I thought he was hiding in Fiji or had started a new life in South America. I didn't think he'd actually be *in stasis* with the treasure we were hunting. I won't let you do this, Benjamin."

His anger began to simmer. "*Let* has nothing to do with it."

Tenzin bared her fangs. "Do you not understand what I'm telling you? I was in stasis. I would have attacked anything that tried to disturb me. It would have been automatic. But Brennus is not resting peacefully in a cave where penitents feed him. He is resting in a barrow of his own making. An ancient king with his wealth gathered around him. He has not set traps to deter thieves, he *is* the trap. All anyone would need to do is disturb his treasure and he would wake. And he would wake hungry."

Ben tapped on a map of the churchyard, an X marked in the spot where the standing stone sat. He'd made notes and taken pictures of its location, but he hadn't connected the stone to the king. He'd been too focused on the well and footprint at Dunino Den.

"Ben, are you listening to me?"

The Raven King was an earth vampire. He could burrow anywhere. And an ancient holy site that had crowned kings and was then protected by new druids—as Brennus probably saw the holy men who founded the church—would have seemed perfect. No one would be disturbing his rest. The earth was verdant. There was water nearby.

"He's not dead." Tenzin's voice rose. "He *will* be hungry. The first thing that unearths him will be food for that hunger. He will be ravenous. Animallike. Out of his senses. There will be no reasoning—"

"We can bring an animal with us," Ben said quietly. "An offering. If he wakes, he'll feed from that."

"If he wakes, he'll want human blood."

"You don't know that."

"I have been in stasis, do you understand?" she shouted. "Leave this alone, Benjamin. I forbid it."

He glared at her. "You don't get to *forbid* me from doing anything," he said. "I am not your servant. I am your partner. And if I think the risk of trying for the sword is worth it—"

"Don't you understand?" Her eyes were wild. "It's just treasure! It's a *metal sword*. There are a million swords in the world. They are like stars in the sky."

"Says the woman who has a reputation to fear and the wealth to back it up. I'm not you, Tenzin. I need this."

"This treasure is not worth your life when you are so fragile."

"So now I'm fragile?" He sneered.

She flew over the table and grabbed him by the shirtfront. "You know what I mean!"

"And you know why I need to do this!"

She was hovering over him, her face inches from his, but Ben refused to be intimidated. Her fangs had cut her bottom lip, and he could smell the metallic scent of her blood. Her fingers were cool against his neck, but her breath was hot.

"I am not yours to command," he whispered.

Tenzin was not his mistress. Not his employer. He brought just as much to this business as she did, and this was *his* job, not hers.

"You're insane," she said, shoving him back and returning to her chair.

"No, just determined. And flexible. I received new information about the mark—thank you very much—but I'm not giving up the job."

"This is not a con."

"I know that."

"Brennus will kill you."

"Or maybe I'll kill him."

Tenzin snarled. "Foolish boy! Do you think I have no honor? Brennus is a warrior of legend. Father of your friends. Do you think I would let you slay him while he rests?"

"Is he an honorable warrior or an animal with no reason?" Ben asked. "You can't have it both ways, Tiny. If he attacks me, I'll defend myself."

"And you'll die."

"Says you."

"Says common sense," Tenzin said. "You're not thinking clearly. You're too focused on the gold. You need to—"

"You need to stop treating me as a child," he said. "I'm not one. You think I've never stolen anything from someone more powerful and dangerous than me? Think again."

"Not. Brennus."

"You don't even know this vampire."

"I know his type."

Ben took a deep breath and closed his eyes. "This is useless. I'm not asking your permission. I'll dig during the day. It'll offer another layer of protection. If Brennus wakes—"

"And you think the church is just going to let you dig up the area under a historic standing stone for... what? Fun? Bribes? What's your plan here?" she asked. "You need to have permission to dig during the day. I'm not going to be with you, so we can't use amnis."

He paused and thought. She had a point. He couldn't dig during the day without attracting human attention. The area was sparsely populated, but it wasn't deserted. And he couldn't dig at night, not when the monsters had free run of the countryside.

"Dawn and dusk," Ben said. "I'll scout the location today at dusk. Before the sun goes down. Get a reading on how deep it is, then come back just before dawn and dig. It can't be that deep, and he's in stasis. He might even be sleeping. Not everyone is a day walker."

"You're a fool," Tenzin said.

He waited, because calling him a fool wasn't saying no. And Ben knew Tenzin was partly right. This was his job, but he still needed her help.

"If you're determined to do this," she said, "dawn and dusk are the only times that might work."

He was wary of her agreement. "So you're coming with me?"

"After the sun goes down?" Tenzin sat back down, her arms crossed over her chest. "Of course I'm coming with you. You're my partner. And I'm your only chance of not getting killed."

BEN DRESSED and put on his boots, grabbing the last of the sunlight while he could. He left a disapproving Tenzin at the cottage and followed the stream up the wooded path that led to the church, his metal detector bulky under his coat. He'd gotten a few odd looks over the past week, but nothing from anyone who wasn't a passerby. None of the few residents in the area seemed to pay him any mind. And though he'd walked around the churchyard, he hadn't once seen anyone coming from the church building.

With that expectation, he was more than a little surprised to interrupt an old woman when he climbed the top of the stone stairs leading up from the glen.

"Hello," he said, a friendly smile plastered on his face. She didn't look like a tourist. Her clothes were old and worn. They looked homemade. "I didn't expect anyone out this late. How are you today?"

The old woman had a stooped back and bright blue eyes. Her hair was tucked under a scarf, but he could see flyaway grey curls escaping the edges.

"I am as I am," she said. "But what are you?"

It was impossible to hide the metal detector from her keen eyes. He shrugged and decided to play it casual. "Just... out for a bit of fun."

She smiled, and he saw she had a tooth missing from the front. "You're another after the Raven King's gold."

"Another?" he asked. "Has someone else been by?"

"Now and then they wander by," she said. "Those of the earth and the air."

Was she talking of the fairy legends surrounding the den? Local legends were part of what had led him to this place, so it wasn't a surprise that she mentioned them. Or was she talking about vampires? *Those of the earth and the air?* There was no way of telling without provoking more questions.

Ben maintained the casual veneer. "So, do you have any advice for the new guy?"

The old woman cackled and pointed to the well where reeds grew long. "Have you made your prayer to the old gods yet?"

His smile fell a little. "I'm not much for praying."

"That's too bad." She stooped down and brought out a pair of trimmers from the pocket of her coat. "A well-placed prayer will never do you wrong." She clipped at some of the greenery around the well. Ben didn't know enough about herbs or botany to know what she was clipping, but she put it in a shallow basket by the edge of the water. "But then, I suppose a machine like you have is very modern."

Something about the woman made him want to linger, but he saw the sun dropping quickly. "Well, you have a good—"

"Don't forget"—the old woman straightened—"be back inside at sundown. No treasure is worth getting snatched and carried away, eh?"

He paused. "What do you mean?"

"Snatched by the Raven King, boy." Her eyes lost some of the merry and bright. "Tales is tales for a reason. Seven years, they say, to be dancing in the Raven King's court. But I've never seen a one return, have you?"

Snatched by the Raven King? Perhaps Brennus wasn't in the kind of stasis Tenzin imagined. "Have people been lost?"

"Here and there," she muttered, bending to her task again. "Seven below, seven on earth, and seven for the people of the air. Everyone knows that."

"Right." Ben didn't usually dismiss folktales, but these sounded like a bastardized explanation for people going missing around Brennus's mound. He'd have to remember to tread carefully. "Well, I'm off. Have a good night."

She waved at him but didn't look again. "Remember,

not after the sun goes down, boy."

"Yeah, thanks. I'll be careful." He turned and walked up the path. Within seconds, the old woman was lost to his vision and nothing but fading sun and green trees surrounded him. He walked the path through the churchyard, looking for the stone he'd earlier dismissed. He caught sight of it and paused to look around before he stepped over the fence.

He circled the stone and turned on the metal detector, casting his eyes again to see if anyone watched him. He felt exposed in the graveyard, the speckled stone monuments watching like silent sentries as he swept the grass with his beeping contraption that felt so very out of place in the still and dimming evening. Just as it had been the past few days, no one interrupted him. No one disturbed him when the heavy mist turned into a drizzle and the machine gave its first beep.

Ben listened with a practiced ear.

Gold.

His heart leapt in his chest, and he itched to find a shovel. A spade. Anything to start digging immediately. But he stopped, paused, and marked the first hit with a golf tee. Then he went back to work, walking a grid around the stone.

He hit again. Another tee.

Again. Another tee.

In the space of twenty minutes, he marked the ground with twelve green tees, barely visible unless you were looking for them. Twelve green tees outlining a circle of roughly twelve feet across. And at the center was the standing stone with the pile of silver coins at the top. The markers backed up what Tenzin had told him.

Benjamin Vecchio had found Brennus the Celt.

7

_____

TENZIN FLEW OVER HIM AFTER the sun had set as he walked back down the stream, over the fields, and toward their temporary home. Some nights Tenzin wondered if Ben realized he lived his life like a vampire. He only rested during the day, when immortals were confined. He did most of his work at night unless he had to visit human establishments. He thought in terms of power dynamics, threats, and allies. He was a vampire in all but biology and durability.

She watched him shut the door of the cottage, then she flew into the woods and checked the rabbit snares she'd set the night before. Seeing two animals hanging in the traps, she grabbed them, stowed the snares in the bushes, and flew back to the house. She cleaned the animals and buried the innards in a shallow hole. Some scavenger would come and dig them up if it had need of them. She eyed the skins but had no real use for them and no method of tanning available at the cottage.

Pity. So much in the modern world was wasted.

Leaving the skins hanging on a fence, she took the

carcasses back to the house and thought about what Ben had in the cupboards. Carrots and potatoes would be enough to add to the rabbits. She'd seen some overgrown herbs in the garden.

She could hear him banging around in the cottage, shucking off his soiled boots and jacket, humming under his breath. His human habits were oddly comforting.

Home. They made her feel at home. It was an odd, but not unwelcome, sensation.

"Ben." She kicked at the door until he opened it. "I found dinner."

He glanced down at the rabbits and raised a curious eyebrow. "So you did." He looked up. "I found Brennus."

She sighed. "Are you sure you're not going to change your mind on this?"

"Positive." He ushered her inside. "What can I do for dinner?"

She'd table the discussion about Brennus's gold until she was feeding him. "How are you at identifying herbs?"

"Uhhhhh." He frowned. "What are herbs again?"

"Ha-ha." She handed him the skinned rabbits.

"Thanks?" He walked them over to the sink.

"Cut those up and put them in a stewpot with some chopped potatoes and carrots," Tenzin said. "I'll get the herbs." She headed for the back door and paused. "I will miss your appetite."

He looked up from the bloody rabbits. "Huh?"

"Nothing."

NOTHING.
Sure, Tenzin.

Ben ignored her sly insinuations about his mortality because it was no good arguing with her. Tenzin was determined that really, secretly, he wanted to be a vampire.

He really, honestly didn't.

The pot was bubbling on the stove and Ben was looking over the diagram he'd drawn in his notebook when he heard the door open. "My best guess, the hoard starts at about a meter down."

"That matches my feeling about the place too." Tenzin walked over to the stove and fiddled with the flame before she threw some green things in. "But it will go deeper."

"Into the sandstone?"

She nodded and stirred the pot. "I need to know if the sword will be enough."

Ben didn't answer too quickly. "I think... if he wasn't living, I'd want it all. At least to recover it. Even if we handed over the majority of the treasure to Max, I'd still want to recover it. But if he's alive, it feels more like stealing."

"But you still want the sword."

"I still want the sword."

"And that's not stealing?"

He let out a long breath. "Yes. But... I'm not keeping it. We can always tell Max to give it back if Brennus decides to return to the world, can't we?"

"We can."

"And as long as we get that one artifact—that one thing —people will know I found the treasure."

Tenzin said, "They're going to wonder where the rest of it is unless we tell them Brennus is living."

He shook his head. "Not our secret to tell."

She smiled and crossed her arms. "You have a very nuanced sense of honesty."

"You probably deserve some credit for that, so don't judge."

"I'm not. I find it entertaining."

He closed his notebook and rose to walk to the kitchen. "We hand the sword over to Max and let people wonder. 'Do they have the treasure? Are they hiding it?' If it works out the way I hope, it'll only get people talking more. We both know how much vampires love to gossip. The more people talk, the more likely they are to hire us."

"If for nothing else than curiosity," Tenzin said.

Ben frowned. "That's fine as long as they pay us too."

"They'll pay us," Tenzin said. "No one cheats me. Being an assassin gave me a reputation for that."

Ben held in a shudder. "Has anyone tried?"

"Yes." She glanced up. "They're dead now."

Why was he not surprised?

THEY ATE. He slept. Ben wanted to be ready to search before the crack of dawn. Tenzin would be able to join him until the sun rose over the horizon, which meant they had a fair amount of light without direct sun. It would be the best time to search, though he'd be vulnerable. He didn't know how long they'd have to dig in order to find the sword. He was only praying that Brennus hadn't followed medieval tradition and buried himself grasping his sword.

If that was the case... Yeah, they were pretty much screwed.

He'd laid out every piece of equipment and checked it twice. Probes and shovels were about as high tech as it got when it came to actually getting gold out of the ground. He briefly debated calling a trusted earth vampire to come move ground, but knew it would just make everything more complicated in the end.

This was something he had to do. Him. Ben Vecchio.

And his mad, miniature partner.

He slept deeply. Tenzin had promised not to leave the cottage until he woke. He dreamed of lying in the sun in the barley fields by the house in Florence. The wool blanket was at his back and the heavy heads of grain bent with the wind, brushing his bare skin as a warm body stretched beside him. Stretched limbs and the scent of honey. He rolled to the side and reached out—

"Ben!"

He woke with a gasp, automatically gathering the sheets around his body. "Dammit, Tiny, I'm naked."

"No, you're not." She patted his cheek. "Wake up."

He blinked and glanced at the clock. "It's not time." His voice croaked, and he coughed to clear it. No sun. No barley field. He was in Scotland, and it was cold and damp and they had to go tromp around in the mud to dig up an early medieval sword.

Ben rubbed his eyes. "Why did you wake me up? My dream was way better than—"

"We have to go. Someone is at Brennus's barrow."

"*What?*"

BY THE TIME he reached the churchyard, Tenzin was already there, staring down at a pit opened in the field next to the standing stone.

"What the hell?" he muttered. He still felt half-asleep, and this was like a dream. The moon was full and low in the sky and a drifting fog covered it, making the whole graveyard glow with an unholy light. Tenzin stood in the moonlight, her hair loose around her shoulders. She hovered over the ground, examining the pit.

Ben ran up to her, barely stopping before he fell in. "Who is it? How did they find the site? Is it gone? What happened?"

Tenzin glared and held up one of the golf tees. "Did you have to put out a flag?"

"A flag?" His mouth dropped. "Those? You could barely see them in the grass."

"No, *you* could barely see them, human. But you're not an earth vampire, are you?"

Well, an earth vampire would certainly explain the giant hole in the ground. Most of them could move dirt like Ben moved furniture. The edges of the pit were smooth. The sides were steep. He resisted the urge to dig through the loose piles of dirt that cluttered the grass.

He couldn't see down into the darkness of the mud and mist. "Who is it?"

"*Merde.*" A quiet, desperate curse drifted from the bottom of the pit.

Ben and Tenzin exchanged a look.

"René," he said.

"René."

"Stop staring," René hissed from the bottom of the pit. "Help. Me."

Ben put his hands on his hips. "Do you think he found Brennus?"

"Oh yeah."

"Do you smell any blood?"

"Not yet," Tenzin said. "There is a not-surprising amount of... restless energy, however. It's only a matter of time."

"So he's not awake?"

Quiet, whispered curses in French met Ben's ears. Apparently René didn't appreciate their casual conversation at the edge of his grave.

"Well, that's what you get for trying to steal my treasure," Ben said. "Think twice next time, René."

"You bastard human piece of *aaaargh*—"

Tenzin said, "I think Brennus is awake."

A strangled, gargling sound came from the bottom of the pit. Ben backed away slowly, but Tenzin's hand shot out and grabbed his arm.

"Don't run," she said calmly. "Stay right where you are."

"Are you nuts?"

"You can't see him, but he's watching you. If you run, he'll chase you."

Ben couldn't pull away. She had his arm in an iron grasp. A scraping sound came from the pit. Then the earth moved beneath him, and the ground bulged like a fountain churning living soil.

Rising from the darkness was a hunched figure with dirty auburn braids falling down his back. He was lean, nearly skeletal, and his skin was marked with swirling patterns and spiral scars. He hunched over a kicking figure that was struggling to break from the iron grasp of the monster who held him.

Brennus the Celt was feeding from René. As Ben and Tenzin watched, his flesh swelled and filled in, like a dry sponge soaking in water. René kicked and twisted, but Brennus didn't seem to notice, nor did he release the vampire from his grasp.

Ben had never seen anything more frightening.

"We should stop this," Tenzin said.

"Why?" Ben whispered. "In the grand scheme of things, it's him or us and I vote for—"

"Brennus." Tenzin's blade was at her side.

Shit!

She called in Latin, "*Ecce tuum sanguis.*" Behold your blood.

The monster paused, flexed his shoulders, and turned toward Tenzin. But instead of Tenzin, his eyes locked on Ben.

Well, that was sadly predictable.

With a curled lip and a snarl, the emaciated vampire leapt from the earthen pit and attacked. Ben didn't even feel him collide. He was standing; he was on his back.

Brennus was poised over Ben, his fangs bared. Blood dripped into the gnarled red-brown beard that fell down the ancient's tattooed chest. But while he crouched over Ben, his head was yanked back and a bronze blade pressed against his throat. Ben blinked to clear the dirt from his eyes. He tried to take a breath, but the ancient's weight lay on his chest, his hands planted by Ben's shoulders. Brennus snarled and snapped his teeth but was held back by Tenzin's grip and the sword at his neck.

Tenzin continued in Latin. "This one is *not* your blood."

Brennus blinked, and Ben saw a shadow of reason return to vivid blue eyes.

"*Sida,*" he growled in a cracked voice.

"We don't use that name anymore, old man."

It was both fascinating and frightening to behold. As Ben watched, Brennus's cheeks grew less hollow and his lips plumped red as René's blood worked through his system. Ben began to see a shadow of the king he must have been. He wasn't as old as he'd first appeared. Perhaps forty in human years. He was barrel-chested and shorter than Ben, though probably tall for the men of his time.

"Why have you woken me?" Brennus managed to croak out, also in Latin. At the movement of his throat, Tenzin's blade pressed into the flesh. It sliced, but no blood dripped out. The vampire had none to spare.

"We did not wake you. A child of your blood did that."

Brennus's lip curled like a great hunting cat; his eyes still locked on Ben's neck. "You are not of my blood. Why are you here?"

Ben knew the question was directed at him. Brennus might have been mad with hunger, but he wasn't completely without reason. Ben reached down, managing to work his hand into the pocket of his trousers and grab the gold coin he'd collected from the streambed days before.

"I come to pay tribute"—he held the gold coin in front of Brennus's eyes—"at the Raven King's stone."

Brennus blinked. "Ravens like ribbons...," he muttered.

"But they like silver more." Ever so slowly, Ben scooted away from Brennus. He wiggled out from under the vampire's body and knelt on the grass. He didn't run. He held the gold in front of the vampire, who watched the coin as it glittered in the moonlight.

"Can I offer my gold to the Raven King?" Ben flipped the coin over, and Brennus blinked.

Abruptly, the vampire's eyes moved from the coin to Ben's face. "Who are you, mortal?"

More and more reason returned to his eyes.

"I'm the son of a scholar," Ben said. "But I am seeking the Sanguine Raptor." He caught himself. "The *Fitheach Lann*," he said. "I came looking for the Raven's blade."

"What need have you of my sword?" Brennus asked. "Are you a knight?"

They were still speaking in Latin, and Ben had never been more grateful that his uncle considered it God's language. At the time Brennus was buried, his English—if he even spoke it—would have been barely recognizable to Ben's modern ears.

"I seek the blade for one of your children," he said.

"That one?" Brennus curled his lip and nodded toward René, who was groaning and twisting in the dirt.

"No. The one I serve is the son of Carwyn ap Bryn, who is the son of Maelona, your child."

A flicker of recognition. "This vampire is the son of Maelona's child?"

"Yes."

Something worked behind Brennus's eyes, and Ben caught a flicker of who the old king might have been when reason still ruled him.

"How fares my daughter, mortal? Do you serve her as well?"

Well, shit. This probably wasn't going to end well.

"Maelona walked toward the dawn," Tenzin said before Ben could speak. "She had joy in her life and in her blood. She only looked for peace."

Tears filled Brennus's eyes and dripped down his cheeks.

Ben said, "But Maelona's son is alive, and he sired many children. And they sired children. Your clan is all over the world now."

"I care nothing for conquest," Brennus said. "I only wish to rest in the earth." Brennus blinked and his head darted up. His nostrils twitched and his eyes closed. "There is a creature roaming the woods. Release me, sida. I will hunt this beast and regain my strength."

"Will you attack this mortal?"

"I give you my word I will not."

Tenzin caught Ben's eye and he nodded. Slowly, he rose and walked to Tenzin's side. When Ben reached her, Tenzin released Brennus, who ran into the dark woods without a backward glance.

"Please tell me it's a deer out there," Ben said.

"Pretty sure. Though Brennus may end up hunting cows for all we know."

A low moaning sound caused them both to turn.

"Are you still on the ground?" Tenzin asked.

René rolled over and Ben winced. The vampire's throat looked like mangled meat. His neck had been gnawed on, and his face was pale from blood loss.

"Need blood." René's eyes lit on Ben.

"Don't even think about it," Tenzin said. "You've caused enough trouble tonight."

"How was I supposed to know he was alive?" René's voice was barely more than a wheezing rasp. He wouldn't heal until he got some blood, but Ben didn't have any urge to help him out. He didn't even let Tenzin drink from him, not that she needed blood very often at her age.

"How were you supposed to know he was alive?" Ben asked. "By doing your research, asshole. And not just following after us like a dog looking for scraps."

Despite his pale face, René curled his lip and bared his fangs.

"Give it up, René," Tenzin said. "I hardly think this performance is going to impress the Ankers."

Ben cocked his head. "Is that who he's working for? But why would they want—"

"Tell you later," Tenzin said. "Besides, René doesn't care what the Ankers wanted the sword for, do you René? This was just a job to you."

Ben said, "He's hired help. And not very good at it."

The hate flared in René's eyes, but Ben was feeling cocky with the vampire on the ground. He squatted next to the Frenchman, close enough to taunt him but far enough to stay out of grabbing distance. "If you're very nice, I'm sure Tenzin can fly to the house and get some blood-wine for you."

René looked between Ben and Tenzin, then he nodded slowly.

"But you're not getting the good stuff," she said. "I don't like you that much." Then she knelt over him and plunged her blade into his shoulder, digging it into the ground and pinning René to the grass as he screamed in pain. "I can't trust you to be civilized when you're this injured. I know you'll understand when you're more rational."

Tenzin flew off, and Ben sat waiting in the cold churchyard, a giant pit on one side, a cursing vampire on the other, and a ravenous ancient hunting in the woods.

Well, he definitely wasn't bored.

René continued to spew vile threats, but Ben had seen how deeply Tenzin's blade had penetrated. René wasn't getting off the ground, especially as weak as he was from blood loss.

And considering what was hunting in the woods, Ben knew he should probably be more worried.

Thanks, adrenalin.

A few minutes later, Ben heard rustling in the bushes. He placed his hand on his hunting knife and took deliberate breaths to calm his pulse as Brennus walked out of the trees. His tension eased as the vampire drew nearer.

Brennus was no longer the hunched figure that had emerged from the earth. His skin was flushed and his red hair and beard dripped with water. He must have splashed in the stream, because though his chest and arm muscles were filled in, Ben didn't see a drop of blood.

More important to Ben, reason had returned to the vampire's arresting gaze. He stood at the edge of the church-yard, surveying the land and watching the human and vampire who stood before him. He frowned at the pinned René.

"Is there a reason he has a sword in his shoulder?"

Brennus was still speaking Latin, so Ben replied in kind. "Tenzin went to get him some blood. She didn't trust him not to kill me."

"She is wise," Brennus said. "Are you a day servant for the sida?"

"You mean Tenzin?"

"Yes."

Ben made a mental note to look up the word *sida*.

"I'm her partner," Ben said. "We work and travel together."

Brennus nodded. "In my time, it was not common for our kind to copulate with humans, though perhaps it is more acceptable now."

"What? No! No, it's not like that."

Brennus looked skeptical. "Truly? Because I thought..."

"Nope."

"Are you sure?"

Ben blinked. "Yes. Quite sure."

"Because she's very possessive."

"I'm her *partner*."

"I see," Brennus said, still looking unconvinced. He stretched out his arms and twisted his torso like an athlete warming his muscles. "Well, the world is always changing. What year do they call it now? Who is the human king?

What language does he speak? And by what name shall I call you?"

Ben tried to sort through the barrage of questions. "No king," he said. "Not right now anyway. Uh... most nations are kind of past the whole king thing."

Brennus frowned. "No kings?"

"Nope. We're trying democracy right now."

Brennus snorted. "Good luck to you."

"And my name is Benjamin Vecchio. So I guess you can call me that."

"Well met, Benjamin Vecchio. In my time I had many human slaves, and I rarely killed them. Humans were protected in my household and considered honorable and necessary."

Really?

"That's... good to hear," Ben said. "But I am not Tenzin's slave."

"Where did your partner—as you call her—go to hunt?"

"Not far. I'm sure she'll be back soon." Ben gestured at René. "He's not in good shape."

"He will live." Brennus went down on one knee and patted René's shoulder. "My thanks, blood of my blood. You have fed your sire and restored him to health. The honor is yours."

Ben noticed how grateful René looked.

So, *so* grateful.

He bit back a smile as Tenzin landed, carrying a bottle of the blood-wine she'd ordered in London.

Brennus said, "Ah sida, your... partner was just informing me that this land has no king."

"No, it has a queen, but she is nothing but a puppet. Common people make the laws and enforce them."

Brennus shook his head. "Madness."

"I know," Tenzin said. "I try not to think about it too much."

Brennus motioned to René. "What shall I do with this one?"

"He is of your line," Tenzin said. "I have brought blood to heal him, but you may do with him what you would. He *is* the one who woke you from your rest." She glanced at Ben.

Okay, yes. Clearly, waking an ancient vampire from sleep was a bad thing. Lesson learned.

René's eyes looked panicked for a second before his face turned stoic. He looked... resigned. Ben almost felt sorry for him.

"Despite his unwise actions, I approve of his courage," Brennus said. "Though he disturbed me, I will let him live."

Tenzin held the bottle of blood-wine toward René but pulled it back at the last second. René whimpered.

"Brennus," she said. "I would offer this blood-wine to you first. It is only proper."

"You honor me," Brennus said. "But I have no desire for wine."

"It is blood preserved with wine."

"Blood preserved in a glass bottle?"

"It keeps for many years," Tenzin said. "No rotting or spoiling."

"I must try this blood." Brennus took the bottle, tipped it up, and took a drink. He smiled. "That is far more pleasant than whatever beast I drank from in the field."

"Probably a cow," Ben muttered.

"Indeed not," Brennus said. "For the blood of the cow is second only to the blood of man. This was a strange and hairy white beast with a long neck and unpleasant disposition."

Oh shit. Well, the neighbors' llamas had lived a long life. Probably.

"But this blood-wine is excellent. *Most* excellent." Brennus crossed his arms and narrowed his eyes, watching as Tenzin bent down and offered the rest of the wine to René. "So, Benjamin Vecchio, tell me why you were here when I woke from my rest."

Ben said, "As I told you, I came to look for your sword." *And steal it.*

"Because one of my line has need of it?"

In a very loose sense... "Yes."

"Very well." Brennus inclined his head regally. "I will consider your offer. What will you give me in exchange for the use of my sword?"

Well... damn. What did he have to offer a legendary immortal Celtic king?

A metal detector?

Money?

"Uh..." Ben had a feeling none of those things were going to impress Brennus very much. He looked desperately at Tenzin, who was trying to tell him something with her eyes, but it wasn't making any sense.

He'd found the Sanguine Raptor. He had survived the ancient vampire who guarded it.

Now how on earth was he going to keep it?

8

_____

POOR BEN. HE LOOKED SO confused. Didn't he realize Brennus had already told him what he wanted? Should she let him dangle for a while longer or just make the offer herself? It had clearly slipped Ben's notice.

She waited a few more beats. Just when Ben started to look truly desperate and Brennus started to look annoyed, she decided she'd waited long enough.

Besides, the Frenchman was starting to knit back together. In a few minutes, he'd be able to talk.

"A case of the wine," Tenzin said. "Twelve bottles. Nearly the blood-weight of two humans. Think of it, Brennus. You can keep this wine with you as you rest. When you wake, you will be able to drink as you will and rise in control of your hunger."

It was exactly what the old vampire had been thinking. Tenzin knew, because it was one of the first things that occurred to her when she first consumed blood-wine.

Brennus smiled and nodded at her. "Very well. I will give loan of my sword to this human if he vows to pass it into the safekeeping of my kin in exchange for this fine wine you have shared with me tonight." He looked around. "This world is not to my liking. I believe I will retire again."

René finally rose to his feet, holding his throat as he spoke in a rasping voice. "Chief Brennus, father of my line, pay no attention to this human. *I* am your kin. I am René, son of Luc, son of Carwyn, son of Maelona. I also seek the Sanguine Raptor."

Ben said, "But he works for one outside your bloodline. He only wants the sword to get rich."

"Is this true?" Brennus asked.

René glared at Ben. "No more than this one seeks the sword for his own glory. He is a hired thief, nothing more."

Brennus looked at Ben. "Were you given money to seek the Raven King's blade?"

Tenzin wanted to speak, but Ben's expression was calm and confident. He stepped forward and held out the gold coin he'd first used to captivate Brennus when he'd been out of his wits.

Something in Tenzin's chest ached. Ben stood, bold as a crow, smiling in the face of an immortal just barely in control. Maybe it was naiveté. Maybe it was pure guts. But there he stood, holding a token out to the legendary king like a knight on a quest. He didn't look away. Didn't shy from Brennus's power.

"I was offered a token," Ben said. "A gesture of good faith like the token I offered at the Raven King's stone."

Brennus said, "For if there is nothing staked, then what do we risk?"

"Exactly," Ben said. "Brennus, I give you my *word* that I will put your sword in the hand of the one who shares your blood. Who wants it to protect and *not* to sell as treasure." His hand held steady, the gold coin in his palm.

Brennus paused and looked between Ben with his

bright face and outstretched palm, and René, holding his neck with a wary expression and blood dripping between his fingers.

He put his palm over Ben's coin. "My faith is in you. I will have your word on this gold that when I rise again, the Sanguine Raptor will find its way back to me."

She saw the brief hesitation. Saw Brennus's reaction to it. The old vampire understood in an instant what Ben thought but wouldn't say. *Would Ben still be alive when the Raven King finally woke?*

A slight smile touched Brennus's lips. "Mortal, your fate is clear to all but you."

Ben said, "I give you my word. I will do everything in my power to return your sword to you. And I will leave it in hands I trust."

Brennus nodded. "Very well, human. We have an agreement between us."

René shouted, "What is this?"

Brennus pinned him with a single look. René fell silent, but his eyes remained on Ben.

Nothing good would come of this. Though they had saved his life, Ben had made an enemy and bested René at a game the Frenchman thought he'd walked into as a winner. Tenzin would have to keep an eye on René Dupont. No doubt he'd be keeping an eye on them.

Brennus reached down and plunged his arm into the soil. The earth rippled and flexed beneath his hand. Then, slowly, the ancient king pulled the Sanguine Raptor, the raven's blade, from the old churchyard in Dunino Den. The blade was blackened iron, its single edge curved like the line of a horse's back. The sharp tip ended less than an arm's length from the hilt, which was a stylized raven with ruby eyes.

Tenzin stared at it and *wanted* it.

Damn Ben Vecchio and his insane idea about professional ethics. The sword Brennus held reminded Tenzin of the falcatas on the Iberian Peninsula.

She didn't have a falcata, and her sword wall was now incomplete.

Brennus held the blade out to Ben, who took it by the hilt, showing the sword the respect it deserved. She'd trained him well.

"Cool your gaze, sida." Brennus's eyes cut to Tenzin. "This blade is not for you."

"A pity," Tenzin said, "for I would wield it well."

"No doubt you would." He held up a finger to Ben. "A loan, human. That is all I will grant you."

Tenzin didn't watch as Ben and Brennus exchanged polite words about the Sanguine Raptor. She didn't listen to the stories Brennus told or the questions Ben asked.

She watched René Dupont. And she waited.

BRENNUS THE CELT, legendary chieftain, warrior of renown, father of one of the largest clans of earth vampires on the planet, sank into the ground with so little fanfare that Ben had to pinch himself to make sure he wasn't dreaming. The immortal sat on the ground, a crate of blood-wine beside him, and nodded at Ben before the ground opened up and swallowed him like a wave taking a swimmer into the deep. For a few moments, the earth shifted and shook. The ground pulled in, constricting the churned dirt until it lay smooth and even with the rest of the graveyard.

Then everything fell silent.

The standing stone where humans had laid offerings sat in the same position, though the earth around it was bare of grass. Ben walked over and placed his hand on the stone. His feet barely made an impression in the dirt. Brennus had disappeared as if he had never risen. If Ben didn't have the raven sword in his hand, he probably would have thought he was dreaming.

He felt a gust of wind at his neck. He turned when he heard the scuffling start behind him. There was a blur of bodies, then everything stopped.

Tenzin straddled René on the ground, one hand on his chest and her bronze blade at his throat. "Don't even think about it."

"That sword is mine," René said. "I am the one descended from Brennus. I unearthed the treasure—"

"After I was the one who found it," Ben said. "You were following in my tracks, René. Don't pretend you did the work on this."

"And don't think I don't feel the weight of gold in your pocket," Tenzin said. "Brennus grabbed you, but not before you took a few trinkets for yourself."

"They are nothing to the Sanguine Raptor."

"That may be," Tenzin said. "But you're not walking away empty-handed."

"I want that sword!"

"Not. Going. To. Happen." Tenzin pressed her blade against the still-healing gnaw marks on René's throat. "You don't want to test me on this, Dupont."

René's eyes cut toward Ben. "You cannot always protect him."

"You're a fool if you think he's an easy target," Tenzin said. "But beyond that, you should know that making an enemy of this man"—she nodded toward Ben—"makes you so many enemies, you don't even want to think about it. Do you know who he is?"

"I know he is the spoiled—" René broke off when the sword pressed harder.

"I don't like it when people insult my friends." She bent over and licked at the line of blood dripping from René's neck. "But if you want me to cut you more, go ahead. You taste good, René." She straddled his body, her hold intimate. "No wonder Brennus drank so much."

René bared his fangs, but his eyes were hot on Tenzin.

He likes it. And so does she.

The quick bite of annoyance stabbed his gut. Ben walked over and pressed the tip of the Sanguine Raptor into the ground near René's ear. Looking down on the vampire, he said, "I won this round. No doubt you'll win others. Don't make us enemies, René. That's not what I want."

"You're so magnanimous when you're the one holding the spoils," René said. "I do wonder if your heart will be so generous when I am the one who wins." His eyes darted to Tenzin, who was still bent over his neck, sniffing. "Can you make her stop doing that?"

"Maybe. I promise nothing. " Ben tapped Tenzin's thigh with the flat of the sword. "Tenzin, he's not dinner. At least, he's not dinner *tonight*."

She looked up, her eyes fixed on René. Her hair fell over her face. Her fangs and lips were red with blood. The Frenchman's eyes locked on her.

"René."

"Yes?"

"Don't threaten my friends," she whispered. "I don't like it."

René nodded a little. "I understand."

Tenzin arched up as she straightened, her movements

unabashedly sexual. Anger twisted in Ben's belly, but he quashed it. Without another word, she floated off René's body and came to rest at Ben's side. René took a deep breath, then he sat up, brushed off his hands, and stood.

He looked at Ben. A little longer at Tenzin. He glanced at the horizon and ran without saying another word.

"Well," Ben said. "He'll be having nightmares about that for a while. Or sex dreams. Could be either."

Tenzin laughed. "He is amusing."

"That's certainly one way to think of him."

The sky was just beginning to glow, and Ben was carrying a sword nearly as long as his arm. He decided taking refuge in the cottage was the right move. He walked back over to Brennus's stone and drew a pound coin from his pocket, placing it on the moss- and lichen-covered rock with the other coins resting there.

A scraping sound near his feet made him look down.

Lying in the dirt was the gold coin Ben had found near the stream days before. He bent down and picked it up, flipping it in his fingers. It was warm, as if someone had been holding the piece of gold in the palm of their hand.

"Thank you," he said quietly. "I will keep this."

The earth said nothing.

"PLEASE."

Tenzin stared at the Sanguine Raptor, her chin in her palms, her eyes pleading with him.

"No."

"Please, please."

Ben twisted the wooden vises to the table in the cottage, then he placed the padded alligator clips in them and set the sword between the rubber tips. "Tenzin," he said, "this sword is being cleaned and taken to Max. I cannot believe what good shape it's in." He shook his head and put his hands on his hips. "I don't even see any rust. This is amazing."

"He probably waxed it."

"Stop pouting. Do you think he had it wrapped? He must have had it wrapped."

"Yes." She was still pouting. "It's beautiful. Please, can I have it? I will give you so much gold."

He forced the smile back. "Aren't you the one who told me there were so many swords in the world?"

"But I don't have one like this. All I'm going to see on my sword wall is the space where this should be." She looked up, her eyes shining. "Please, Benjamin."

He shook his head. "Are you making yourself cry right now? I didn't even know you could do that."

"Dammit, Ben! I really want this sword!"

He laughed. He couldn't help it. He sat down and stared at the Sanguine Raptor. It *was* beautiful. Once he'd had time to examine it, he saw why it was so legendary.

The balance was exquisite, even after two thousand years. The quality of the iron was exceptional; he was going to have to research early Celtic iron forging, because there was something different about the quality of the metal. The hilt was worked with copper and gold details, and the stylized raven's eyes were true rubies. He'd thought they might be garnet, but no. Rubies. Delicious cabochon rubies. It was no wonder Tenzin was trying to guilt him into giving it to her. It would be the crown of her collection.

"I'm not going to lie," he said. "I want to keep it myself. But that's not what we're doing here."

"But Ben"—she floated over and settled on the chair

next to him, leaning into his shoulder—"I have stolen things so much less wonderful than this. This is worth stealing. It's worth pissing off lots of people. You'll be fine. I'll protect you."

"Nope."

She threw her head back and groaned. "This is so much worse than I imagined!"

"Suck it up, partner. You didn't have this reaction to the idol we found. What's going on?"

Tenzin rolled her eyes. "The idol was small and ugly. It didn't have anything shiny on it. It definitely didn't have *rubies*."

"Old-world snob."

"*Rubies*."

"I didn't know you liked rubies so much." He patted her shoulder. "I'll have to remember that."

"I'm thinking of something very painful happening to you right now."

"This was the agreement," he said. "No copies. No duplicates. We return the original artifact to the client without forgeries of any kind. How else will clients trust us to deal straight with them?"

"I have never been known for straight-dealing! You're spoiling my reputation as an unpredictable, chaotic force of nature. This could ruin me."

"So dramatic. I'm sure people will still be terrified of you. And don't forget, we do get to split the finders' fee."

She snorted. "What, the hundred and five whole pounds Max gave you for volunteering to find this sword? Do I even want to know how much money we lost on this job?"

Ben tried not to wince, but it was difficult. "It's coming

out of my trust. Don't worry about it. The boost to our reputation will all be worth it in the end."

It better be. He didn't want to think about how much money he'd lost. Spending months on this research hadn't come cheap. Equipment and paying off archivists didn't come cheap either. Of course, some of those relationships would continue. The next time he was in the UK for work, he'd be able to—

"You know." Tenzin broke into his thoughts. "I bet if I was working with René, *he* would let me keep the sword."

Ben cut his eyes at her. "René would let you do all sorts of things I don't want to know about. But he wouldn't let you keep this sword unless you outbid the original clients. Then he'd stab them in the back to give it to you, making an enemy of the Ankers. What is that about, by the way?"

"I think they wanted it for leverage. I haven't found out why yet. But would it really be so bad to piss off the Ankers? They're nothing but an entire clan of spies. People probably piss them off all the time."

"Since I am human and don't really want to die at the hand of one of their many assassins, yes. Yes, it would be."

She put her head on his shoulder. "I really want the sword, Benjamin."

He patted her dark hair. "Learn to say good-bye, Tiny."

"I'm terrible at saying good-bye to things I love."

Oh Tenzin. Ben sighed, because she was right. Tenzin was a collector. Of things. Of people. It was one of the reasons she tried not to get attached at all.

"I know." He turned and kissed the top of her head. "There will be other swords."

"I bet you say that to all your partners."

"Only you, Tiny. Only you."

9

Edinburgh, Scotland

"YOU FOUND IT," MAX SAID, eyeing the sword with a blank expression. "I didn't think you'd actually find it."

Cathy was staring at the sword in abject horror. "Oh... Not good."

This was so far from the reaction Ben expected, he felt like screaming. He'd showed up at Max and Cathy's town house bursting with pride. He'd waited in the sitting room trying to stay cool, but it was difficult.

He'd found the fucking Sanguine Raptor.

Tenzin had come with him but seemed far more interested in looking at the books on the coffee table than engaging in the conversation. She was still pouting about not being able to keep the sword.

"I don't understand," Ben said. "What's going on? What's not good?"

He'd spent over a week painstakingly cleaning the sword in preparation for handing it over to Max. He'd used dental picks to clean the hilt, tested each of the jewels and cleaned them too. Then he'd coated and waxed the blade. Polished and waxed the hilt. He had a scabbard specially made with stitching that complemented the design of the hilt while still being serviceable.

And he'd fought off Tenzin's pleading the whole time.

Now Max and Cathy were looking at the Sanguine Raptor like it would bite.

"What's the problem, Max?"

The vampire's face was pale. "And you said Brennus is alive? You saw him?"

"Yeah, but like Tenzin said, I wouldn't go trying to find him again. He wasn't real happy about being woken up. He's probably moved his resting place by now, and he's back in stasis. I wouldn't go spreading the news that he's alive or anything."

Ben and Tenzin had debated telling Max, but there was no way of getting around the fact that out of the legendary treasure in Brennus's hoard, they'd only recovered one sword.

Ben knew the sword was more than enough to establish his reputation, but he also didn't want Max thinking he'd been cheated. Now Cathy was rubbing Max's shoulder like someone had died.

"Do you want it?" Cathy asked in a low voice.

"Of course I don't," Max hissed. "I never have. The power you have is more than enough. Ioan knew if our clan amassed more we'd only become a target."

Ben was completely lost.

"You could do it. It would be bloodless. You know the MacGregors—"

"This is not about the MacGregors. It's about me."

"Then we don't tell anyone you have it," she said. "There will be rumors, but we can deny—"

"Are you kidding me?" Ben finally shouted. "What are you talking about?"

Max looked up at him. "Can't you just put it back?"

"Of course I can't put it back! Do you understand what we went through to get it in the first place?"

"You told me you were going after the treasure," Max said. "No one can know—"

"The whole reason I searched for this thing was so vampires *would* know! So they would talk about it. And you're going to act like it's some kind of embarrassment? What is wrong with you guys?"

Max shook his head. "Ben, you don't understand."

"No, *you* don't understand," he said. "You don't understand what it's like trying to make a decent reputation in a world that constantly underestimates you. You don't understand what it's like depending on other people all the time. To live off someone else's success. I worked my ass off to find this thing. I risked my life and I invested money—asking nothing from you but permission—so that I could have a job on my résumé. And not just any job. A massive job. A *legendary* job. And now you tell me you're going to pretend it didn't happen and—"

"Do you understand what you found?" Cathy yelled. The room heated in a second. "Do you know what this sword means?"

"Ben." Max rose and put a hand on Cathy's arm. The room cooled back down. Max's normally gregarious face was lined with worry. He looked... older. Less like himself and more like a vampire to be frightened of.

Max said, "The Sanguine Raptor is not just a sword. It's... Excalibur. It's Durendal. It's Tizona."

"I don't know what that means," Ben said. "It's a *sword*, Max." Ben stepped closer. "It's not like some magical creature appeared out of nowhere and handed it to me out of a lake or..."

Max's eyebrows went up.

Ben put his hand over his face. *"Shit!"*

Max and Cathy were both nodding silently. Tenzin started laughing behind him.

"It's funny," she said, "because it wasn't out of a lake. It was out of the ground. He pulled it out of the ground and gave it to you."

Oh, he was screwed.

Max shook his head. "I didn't think you'd find it. I'm sorry, Ben. I thought you would find treasure. Something that would stoke the legends and make for great stories to spread around. You'd get more work. I'd add a few things to my collection, but nothing... nothing like this. I didn't truly believe it existed until you showed it to me."

Ben closed his eyes and sat on the edge of the sofa. "What does this mean?"

Max lifted the blade from the desk where Ben had placed it and drew it from the scabbard. He held it balanced in his hand, his arm stretched out. Then he brought it closer and looked at the tooled iron, the jeweled hilt.

"It really is extraordinary," he murmured.

Max put it back in the scabbard and walked to the sofa, putting the blade on the table in front of him. Cathy sat at his side. Tenzin put the coffee table book to the side, and Ben turned and slid onto the sofa next to her.

Why couldn't it ever be simple?

"This sword," Max began, "is the sword of the king of Scotland. The vampire king. The Raven King."

"Brennus."

"The king who would return, according to immortal legend among Scotland's vampires. There aren't many of us, but the old ones—including Lord MacGregor—do abide by the tradition. MacGregor has never been crowned or taken any title other than the one he was born with. He's a steward only. On the day the Raven King returns, I have no doubt he will bend his knee and hand over his authority to the bearer of this blade."

Ben shook his head. "It's not my blade."

"Tell me," Max said, "as exactly as you can remember it, what Brennus said to you."

Tenzin asked, "Do you want it in English or Latin?"

Cathy said, "English please."

"Ben said, 'I give you my word that I will put your sword in the hand of the one who shares your blood. Who wants it to protect and *not* to sell as treasure.' And Ben offered Brennus a token. A coin he'd found from Brennus's cache. Then Brennus put his hand over Ben's coin and said, 'My faith is in you. I will have your word on this gold that when I rise again, the Sanguine Raptor will find its way back to me.' And he took the coin."

Despite the seriousness of the situation, Ben found it amusing that Tenzin also included dramatic voices in her retelling. He was also slightly in awe that she remembered their words *exactly*.

"Then Ben was thinking about the fact that he's mortal and will probably be dead when Brennus finally gets around to waking up—"

"You don't know that's what I was thinking," Ben said.

Tenzin gave him a look that clearly said: *Whatever, dude.* Then she continued. "So Brennus said, 'Mortal, your fate is clear to all but you.'" Tenzin turned her eyes back to Ben. "Did you get *that*?"

"Be quiet and finish the story, Tiny."

Cathy held a hand up. "Can I just say that the two of you are fascinating to me? I'm not really sure what's going on, but it's very interesting."

Max said, "Finish *please*."

"So finally Ben said, 'I give you my word. I will do everything in my power to return your sword to you. And I will leave it in hands I trust.' And that was it. Brennus told him they had an agreement and then he gave him the sword and basically disappeared."

"Just that?" Max asked. "There was no exchange or formal pledge?"

"Tenzin bribed him with blood-wine," Ben said. "Other than that, no."

Max let out a long breath, and Cathy patted him on the shoulder. "Sorry, sexy. This one is on you."

Ben said, "What does that mean?"

"It means that Brennus didn't give the blade to *you*," Cathy said. "He gave it to Max with you as Max's agent. If he'd given it to you, then Max could bow out and you'd be stuck being the vampire king of Scotland."

"I'm not a vampire!" Ben said.

Cathy nodded. "It would certainly be an awkward and probably very short reign."

Tenzin said, "I would kill people for you. Just so you know."

"Thanks," Ben said. "So that's the deal? Whoever holds the Sanguine Raptor is the vampire king of Scotland?"

"Yes," Max said. "But I have no desire to be king. William—Lord MacGregor—is an excellent and fair ruler. Gemma is already in power in London. Deirdre and Carwyn have massive influence in Dublin, even though Murphy is in charge. If I was the ruler here, our clan would be far too visible. We would be seen as too powerful and we'd become a target. It was one of the reasons Ioan never sought any kind of position. Gemma is the only one of us interested in ruling, and she's still more of a co-executive than a queen. If I become king here..." He sighed and put his hands over his face. "You see why we cannot reveal that the Sanguine Raptor has been found."

Ben frowned. "No. I really don't. Not at all." The answer was so obvious to Ben he didn't know how Max and Cathy hadn't already thought of it. "All you have to do is tell people that Brennus is alive."

Max's head shot up. "What?"

"Whoever holds the Sanguine Raptor is like... the heir of Brennus, right?"

"Yes."

"But Brennus isn't dead. People just think he is. Which is why immortals have tried to find the sword, right? Because whoever has the sword would be the king."

"Or the queen," Cathy added. "There's no requirement the vampire be male."

Max said, "But you said we shouldn't tell anyone Brennus is alive. You promised—"

"Nothing." Tenzin picked up another coffee table book, this one entitled *Maximum Storage, Medieval Space*. "We didn't promise Brennus we'd keep his secret. I don't think he'd really care if anyone knew. If anyone is foolish enough to try to find him and wake him up, that's on their head."

"And let's be honest," Ben said. "René Dupont will tell his clients that Brennus is alive. It's the only excuse he has for not retrieving the treasure. Word is going to spread."

Cathy turned to Max. "He's right. If Brennus isn't dead, then there's no need for a succession. Edinburgh continues to be ruled by a steward of the absent king, and they can just fight over that position if they want to. William will love it because it cements his authority, and since you're a descendant of Brennus's, you can keep the sword in your own armory. Tavish can guard it. It'll give him an excuse to never leave the estate. He'll be the 'Keeper of the King's blade' or something like that. He'll love it."

Max was rubbing his jaw, but his face didn't look quite as pale. "This could work."

"It will work," Tenzin said, paging through the design book. "Vampires, especially old ones, are highly resistant to change. Cathy, are you the designer here or is Max?"

"Me," Max said. "Why do you ask?"

"I need to hang some weapons," Tenzin said. "And I'm just not sure... I'm looking for ideas."

"What type of weapons? Swords? Spears? Do you have any armor?"

Tenzin sat up straighter. "I do have some very nice Kozane armor from Japan, but it's in storage."

"Really?" Max said. "I'd love to see it. As for weapons, it's always nice to vary your presentation. How many rooms are you thinking of? If you need ideas, you *must* come visit the castle. My brother and I inherited an armory."

Ben watched Tenzin's eyes light up and knew he'd lost her. She'd been obsessing over her wall of swords for weeks, and she'd finally found someone who seemed as enthusiastic as she was about decorating with deadly things.

He turned back to Cathy. "So that's it?"

She nodded. "Leave it to me. Max hates politics, and everyone is afraid of me. I'll smooth things over with William." She grinned. "Congrats, kid. You just found your first big treasure."

"And everyone freaked out about it."

She shrugged. "At least you know it'll get everyone talking."

"That's what I wanted."

Cathy ran her fingertip along the length of the ancient sword. "It's beautiful, Ben. Be proud. Be very proud." She clapped her hands together. "Now, there's just one more step to finish this deal."

"Oh yeah?"

"We've got to drink on it. I hope you like whisky."

Ben smiled. "I knew I'd love this country."

BEN AND TENZIN stayed in Edinburgh for two more weeks. They were present when William, Lord MacGregor, steward of Edinburgh, saw his king's sword for the very first time. Despite their initial fears, MacGregor showed no sign of posturing or political gamesmanship. There was only a quiet wonder at hearing the news that Brennus was alive in the world. The Raven King still lived. If anything, his legend had only grown bigger.

Ben shook MacGregor's hand and accepted the vampire's thanks for the recovery of a national treasure. And... the honorary title.

"You said you wanted a title," Tenzin said. "Well, now you have one."

"Master of Iron doesn't actually mean anything, Tenzin."

"It means we need to work on your sword skills, Benjamin Vecchio, Master of Iron in Lothian."

"It makes me sound like I do laundry."

She rolled her eyes. "It's an honorific to say thank you.

'Scribe of Penglai Island' doesn't really mean I'm a scribe, but that's one of mine."

"Commander of the Altan Wind?"

She cocked her head. "Okay, that one means something, but it's not as polite as Master of Iron."

Tenzin had forced herself to be gracious at the various receptions and parties they attended with Max and Cathy, but Ben caught her eyeing the Sanguine Raptor with covetous glances every time she was in the same room with it.

He probably ought to warn Max about that.

"Why don't you have to get dressed up?" He squirmed in his new kilt. The wool itched against his skin.

"I am dressed up." She looked down at the black pants and tunic. "This is embroidered silk."

"And it looks so much more comfortable than this," he muttered.

"You look very handsome." She adjusted the plaid over his shoulder.

Don't say it...

"All the women will want to have sex with you."

"Thanks, Tenzin."

Despite his discomfort with the breeze on his legs, attending the banquet and accepting the title and ceremonial dirk Lord MacGregor gave him felt... big.

It wasn't just that every immortal in Edinburgh was talking about the recovery of the Sanguine Raptor or the beauty of the historic blade. Ben felt part of something bigger.

He'd found something that was missing and returned it to those who valued it. He'd brought a lost thing home. Ben hadn't realized that would mean something to him, but it did.

Ben and Tenzin attended the banquet in honor of the Raven King's throne where William MacGregor, immortal son of Brennus's most trusted counselor, kissed the blade Max held and pledged to watch over the immortals and humans of Scotland until the time that the Raven King decided to finally return. They danced at midnight in a castle outside the city, and when they left, Ben was a Master of Iron in the Scottish court.

BEN AND TENZIN spent two full weeks at Max's castle in the Highlands. Tenzin forced Ben to take a million pictures while she took notes and nearly swooned over Max's collection of axes. Ben would have said her adoration was embarrassing except that both Max and his cranky brother Tavish seemed slightly besotted with the tiny air vampire with the bronze blade.

They laughed. They talked.

They drank a *lot* of whisky.

"I love this place," Tenzin said one night. They were sitting on the floor of the dagger room.

Yes, there was a room full of daggers. Every size and shape you could imagine. Ben was starting to worry that Tenzin would never want to leave.

"We have to go back to New York," he said.

"But why?" she whined. "I could live here, and you could call Max when you need me for something."

He nudged her shoulder. "You'd miss me too much."

"I would not."

"You would. Also, I don't think Max and Cathy get cable here. No HGTV, Tenzin."

Her eyes went wide.

"I don't think they even have Wi-Fi, so no YouTube either."

Tenzin made a face. "Never mind. I'll just come visit their weapons. Besides, Cara would miss me if I lived here."

"You do know she's not an actual person, don't you? It's an artificial intelligence program. There's not an actual person living in the walls or anything."

Tenzin shook her head. "I hope you don't say that at home. You'll hurt Cara's feelings."

"Not a person. No feelings. Artificial intelligence."

Tenzin rose and gave him a disapproving frown. "I expected more kindness from you, Ben."

"Are you joking? I can't tell if you're joking."

She walked out of the dagger room.

"Tenzin?"

Yeah, it was definitely time to go home.

EPILOGUE

BEN FLIPPED THROUGH A MAGAZINE while Tenzin placed the last sword at the top of the wall.

He flipped again.

She floated down to the ground and surveyed her handiwork. She'd have to make Ben take pictures and send some to both Max and Gemma. The two had been instrumental in the overall design scheme of the loft. Both had urged her to retrieve her armor and shields from storage, and the Ngoni and Indian shields made excellent additions.

Maybe she could convince Ben to build a dagger room in the loft.

He let out a small huffing sigh and flipped another magazine page.

Tenzin's eye twitched. "Cara," she called. "Please play music."

"What music would you like?"

"Enya, please. Just play all the Enya you have access to."

Tenzin found there was nothing that induced rage in Ben faster than the soothing sounds of the Irish singer. But lately, anything was better than Ben's silent pouting.

"Cara, stop music," Ben growled.

"Cara, play Enya."

"I do not understand," Cara's smooth lilt intoned. "What music would you like me to play?"

"Enya." Tenzin stared at Ben. "Shuffle. All."

Ben threw down the magazine as a wave of New Age voices filled the room. "What is wrong with you? You know I hate that music."

She batted her eyes at him. "You seem tense."

"I'm fine."

"Really? Because you seem tense." She gestured at the wall. "You haven't even complimented my decorating."

She was quite pleased with the contractor Cara had found. He wasn't cheap, but he was fast and he didn't ask inconvenient questions. Over the past month, she'd planned and placed most of her sword and shield collection. Her armor had been unpacked and mounted in the corners of the loft. Tenzin found she quite liked the idea of hollow warriors guarding their territory. She hoped it would make guests uncomfortable enough that they wouldn't stay long.

"Well?" she asked, gesturing to the length of the wall. "I think Ruben and I are going to start on a conservatory for the roof garden next."

He picked up the magazine again. "That's not decorating. That's easy access to things that can kill your enemies. Useful, I'll grant you, but you're not exactly curating Monet."

Tenzin narrowed her eyes and flew over to Ben, picking him up by the back of his shirt and hoisting him into the air while he kicked and twisted.

"Put me down!"

Flying with Ben when he cooperated was a challenge.

Flying him when he was trying to twist away was almost impossible.

"Do you want to break your legs?" She nearly dropped him. "Stop flailing like a child."

"Put me down, Tenzin!"

She tossed him into her alcove and threw the magazine he was still clutching to the ground.

"You will stop this," she said, glaring at him. "Or I will hurt you."

Ben was red in the face, but he couldn't quell the urge to look around her small loft area. "This is smaller than I thought."

"I am not a very big person."

His head almost touched the ceiling. The loft itself was just over six feet tall and open to the rest of the house, but curtains were hung for when she needed privacy. There was a railing but no ladder. The only way to get in was to fly. There was a simple pallet on the floor with rugs and furs from her home in Tibet. There was an altar in the corner where she meditated and lit incense, and a small loom she'd built. Other than that, it was empty save for a few piles of books.

"Sit," she said.

Ben sat. His eyes were drawn to the loom. "You weave."

"Yes."

He stared at the blank wall across from him. "I didn't know that."

"There's a lot you don't know about me, Benjamin."

He was silent again.

"Why are you so angry?" she asked. "You're making everyone around you miserable."

"The only person I see is you."

"Not true." *Wait, was it?* "Don't dismiss Cara. She's a part of this family too."

At least that made him crack a smile.

Thinking back, Tenzin realized he'd rarely left the loft during the previous month. While she'd been video-chatting with Max and Gemma, ordering around Ruben the contractor, and seeing to the decoration of the loft, he'd been brooding in his office. She didn't know if there were pictures on his walls, and he still hadn't unpacked his books.

"Ben," she asked. "When did I become the well-adjusted one?"

"I don't know," he said. "It's so wrong."

"It is. I am the strange, frightening vampire and you are the human that everyone likes. This partnership isn't going to work if we try changing that now."

He nodded.

"You need to get a life here," she said. "Make friends. I don't need many people, but I'm not you. The O'Briens have invited you over on several occasions. You need to stop making excuses."

The O'Briens were the immortals in charge of New York City. They were an unruly clan of earth vampires who distrusted most outsiders but had been cautiously friendly to Ben because of his connections to Carwyn in Ireland.

Also, he had money. Which they liked.

She said, "You can only make work excuses for so long when you're not working."

Bingo. The pained look on his face told her what was really bothering him.

"They're going to call," she said.

"You keep saying that"—he picked at the edge of her rug —"but it's been a month."

"A month, Ben. A *month*. You are working with

vampires here. Think about how most of us perceive time. A month is nothing."

He groaned and banged his head against the wall. "This is driving me crazy."

"You don't need the money. Not really. But you do need to relax."

"I don't know how to do that," he said. "My whole life has been busy. School. Training. Studying. Working with Giovanni. More training. More studying."

"Do you think Gio works all the time?"

"Yes." Ben shrugged. "He works as much as he wants."

"*Now* he does. But when we were working together, there were some times where we'd only work three or four months out of the year. That's contract work, Ben. Sometimes you wait for work. Sometimes you wait a long time. And other times you'll have jobs coming from everywhere."

"So how do you deal with it?"

"If you're a hermit like me, you don't care." She shrugged. "If you're *you*, you… go to a party with the O'Briens. Or fly to LA for a few weeks. Travel to Rome and see Fabi. Drink whisky with Gavin. But you *leave the house*."

He sighed.

"Or…," she said. "I'm going to physically hurt you at some point."

He smiled. "Got it."

She nodded toward the ledge. "Get out of my loft. It's too crowded up here with you in it."

He looked over the edge. "Sorry, but unless you have a rope ladder, you're going to have to help me down. I'm not breaking my legs because you had a temper tantrum." He raised his voice. "And for God's sake, Cara, stop playing Enya!"

"Stopping shuffle now," Cara said.

Ben shook his head, muttering, "Passive-aggressive New Age music" under his breath. "Cara," he said, "play the Real McKenzies. Shuffle all. Volume level forty-five."

In a few seconds, the sound of pounding drums and angry bagpipes blasted through the loft.

Tenzin grinned. "This is like the music in the pub!"

"I know!" he shouted. "Now will you get me down from here?"

She flew them both down to the main level and set Ben on his feet.

"Don't pick me up again," he said. "You know I hate that."

"Are you going to stop pouting?"

"I was not—"

"This is Cara." Cara paused the music; her voice—the volume still turned up to forty-five—filled the room. "You have an incoming call from Daniel Preston in York, United Kingdom. Shall I accept?"

Ben frowned. "Do you know a Daniel Preston?"

"No," Tenzin said. "But I have a feeling that he knows you."

Ben's smile lit up the room. "Cara, accept call."

THE END
of the beginning

A NOTE FOR READERS

January 25, 2017

Dear Readers,

There you have it; it's the end of the beginning. I hope you enjoyed Ben and Tenzin's most recent adventure and look forward to their first full novel, which I'll be writing later this year.

I knew four years ago that to write their series, I needed to take some time. I needed to let the characters grow and change. I needed to move them exactly where they needed to be. Ben needed to get older and wiser. Tenzin needed to become a bit (a very little bit) more human and connected with the world.

And here they are.

I hope you've enjoyed the journey so far. Don't worry, there's lots more to come.

A Note for Readers

Thanks for reading,
　Elizabeth

Continue reading for a preview of the first full Elemental Legacy novel
MIDNIGHT LABYRINTH
available everywhere November 7, 2017.

He chased his quarry up the ladder, launching himself onto the gravel-strewn roof in Hell's Kitchen. Ducking under a broken scaffold, he followed the dark figure who threatened to elude him. She was half his size, dressed in a black hoodie and leggings. She moved like a cat in the dim, pre-dawn light.

She was getting away.

He ran left, skimming the side of a cinderblock building before he leapt across a narrow vent, using longer legs to his advantage. He landed hard, rolled in a single somersault, then took to his feet in one smooth movement. He could feel gravel in the small of his back, and his arm was bleeding from the bite of a rusted ladder, but he kept running.

He was gaining on her. He scanned the landscape as he'd been taught, mentally calculating the most efficient way to get from his position to hers.

His lungs pumped in steady rhythm. In-in-out. He pulled in the humid air and tried not to choke. He'd been running at seven thousand feet the week before. His thin black shirt stuck to his skin. Grey light filtered over a city that still clung to the memory of the previous day's heat. New York City in July. Another day; another sauna.

The small figure scrambled up the side of a building—sticking to the stained brick like a spider—then she disappeared over the edge and into nothing.

He wasn't concerned for her safety.

He found the lips of the bricks she'd used to climb. He wasn't as fast as she was. He was forced to take his time crawling up the side of the building, finding each finger hold and jutting brick to move his body up the wall. From a distance, he'd appear to be sticking too. He felt a fingernail tear, but he didn't pause.

Hoisting his body over the edge of the wall, he kept himself low and scanned the urban landscape. Water towers and rusted fire-escapes mixed with recently gentrified gardens and sleek patio furniture.

She was barely visible in the distance, leaping from the top of one building to the next.

He ran after her, but he knew it was futile. She'd gained too much ground during his careful climb. She disappeared over the side of another building and Ben knew he'd lost her.

Panting, he followed her tracks, not allowing himself to slow down. He leapt over the edge of a familiar building and jumped fire-escape railings five stories down until he hung on the last rung of the old ironwork.

Ben Vecchio closed his eyes and did three rapid pull-ups, pushing his muscles right to the edge of exhaustion before he gave them a break. He had a runner's build, but he was six feet tall. Moving a large frame quickly would always be a challenge. He dropped to the ground and jogged down West 47th Street to the deserted playground. The gate was locked, but he easily jumped over.

She'd taught him that trick early.

A small hooded figure perched on the top of a red and green play structure. Still breathing deeply, Ben jumped to the first platform and squatted in front of her.

"Believe it or not, you are getting faster," Zoots said.

"That wall nearly killed me." With the adrenaline waning, Ben was starting to feel his hands.

"But you made it up. That's a ten foot brick wall and you climbed it."

"Slowly."

"But you climbed it," Zoots said. "Remember, I grew up here. I know every inch of those roofs. I have the advantage."

He shook his head. "Doesn't matter. I have to be faster."

It had to be more instinctive. He wouldn't have the luxury of running in familiar places.

Zoots rolled her eyes and pulled out a cigarette. "Whatever, man."

When he'd first moved to New York, he'd watched. There were parkour and free-running groups, but they were cliquish and Ben was a beginner. Though he'd been drilled in martial arts and weapons training since he was twelve-years-old, parkour was new to him. It was only the lightning-quick reflexes of a girl he'd met a few years ago that had attracted him to the practice. She'd moved inhumanly fast.

Of course, she hadn't been strictly human.

Ben was. The sweat dripping into his eyes proved it. He wiped it away and sat next to Zoots.

He'd found her by watching. She wasn't part of the group, but they knew her. She was the one they wandered over to talk to when they were practicing. Zoots was tiny—barely five feet tall—with a slight figure. Her skin was pale under her hood. Her short hair and her eyes were dark. She came out in the early morning and at night. He'd never seen her in the middle of the day.

It had taken Ben weeks to figure out who she was and what she was to the runners in Central Park. If the young traceurs in the park had a guru, it was Zoots. She claimed to be self-taught from YouTube videos, but Ben suspected that Zoots was like him. He'd been running since he could remember, mostly to get away from trouble. She was just better at it.

Zoots ran everywhere, and she was a loner. She ignored Ben for weeks, until her curiosity got the better of her. She'd talked to him, and he'd eventually hired her. He wanted to learn parkour, but he wasn't interested in joining any group. Zoots nodded and told Ben to meet her at Hell's Kitchen Playground and to bring two hundred bucks cash.

So he did.

She finished her cigarette, flicked off the cherry, and carefully tucked the butt into a tin she kept in her pocket. "Same time next week?"

"Yeah."

"You've been doing this for six months now. You know the basics. You sure you want to keep paying me for lessons?"

Ben raised an eyebrow. "You trying to get rid of me, Zoots?"

"It's your money, man." She smiled. "I just spend it."

"I need to be faster."

She eyed him. "That's practice. You're twice my size; you gotta figure out your own style. Tall means longer legs and longer arms, but it also means more meat to move."

"I'll keep paying you if you keep teaching me."

"Like said, it's your money." Zoots narrowed her eyes. "You told me once you needed to learn this for work."

"I do." His fingers itched for a cigarette. He'd stopped smoking when he was fourteen—his uncle could smell the slightest trace of cigarette smoke—but he still wanted one occasionally. Especially when people started asking personal questions.

"But one of the guys in the park said you were in antiquities or something."

Damn, nosy kids. "Yeah."

Zoots frowned. "You jumping roofs at the museum or something?"

Ben couldn't stop the smile. "I work for private clients."

"Huh." She nodded. "So... you're into some serious Indiana Jones-kinda-shit, huh?"

Ben rose and raked a hand through his hair. "Don't be ridiculous, Zoots. You think I'd look good in a hat?"

He caught the quick flush on her cheeks before he jumped off the play structure and walked toward the gate. "See you next week, Zoots."

"Later, Indiana."

Ben caught the train to Spring Street station, walking toward Broadway and his favorite cafe. He sat at the picnic tables outside Cafe Lilo and watched the growing rush of pedestrians filling the sidewalk. He read a newspaper someone had left behind while he drank coffee and devoured a bagel.

There was no typical crowd at Cafe Lilo, which was one of the reasons Ben liked it. Stock brokers, dog walkers, young parents and college kids all frequented the family-owned cafe. A few tourists came in, but it wasn't a flashy place. That morning delivery and sanitation trucks competed in the narrow streets while a growing crowd of taxis and hired cars dodged between them, heading toward Lower Manhattan.

He flipped to the Arts section of the paper and made a few notes about gallery openings. An auction announcement. A charity gala sponsored by some outfit called Historic New York. A new surrealist exhibit opening at the Museum of Modern Art.

His sunlight quota met, he headed back to the building on Mercer he was still renovating. He'd called the massive, unfinished penthouse home for two years. Both stories had finished floors and the semblance of rooms. The roof garden was a work in progress.

He nodded at the silent doorman, who was known for discretion more than amiability, and took the elevator to the top floor. He had two full floors of the building. He pushed the button for the living area on the top floor, bypassing his office on the floor below.

The place was home. It was office.

Finely honed reflexes were the only thing that saved him from the three inch thick book that dropped from the loft overhead.

The loft could also be a death trap.

He glared up. "What are you doing?" There were books —his books—scattered on the floor under her loft. "Tenzin, what the hell?"

Another book fell flat on the floor to his left.

"Stop throwing my books!"

A dark head poked out, cloaked in carefully placed shadows that protected her from sunlight. "Did you move my swords?" She held out another book, narrowed her eyes, and dropped it.

"Cut it out!" Ben shouted. "And no, I did not move your swords. I swear, Tenzin—"

"Are you sure?" A small figure floated out of the loft like the proverbial angel of book death, arms stretched out with two of his massive art books in her hands. "Are you sure you didn't move my swords?"

Damn, pain-in-the-ass stubborn air vampire.

Ben glared at her. "I did not…"

Oh shit. He had.

"I told you," she said.

"One sword, Tenzin! *One*. Sword." He held his hands out, ready to rescue his books. "Do not drop those books."

Tenzin hovered over him, a pissed-off, flying demon with a pretty, round face and a sheet of black hair falling around her. She looked young, but she wasn't. She was one of the most ancient elemental vampires on the planet, born on the northern steppes of Asia thousands of years before. She was also Ben's partner.

And a book abuser.

She wouldn't have tried it when she'd been working with his uncle, Giovanni Vecchio. Of course, Giovanni was a rare book collector and a fire vampire who would have seriously wounded her if she tried.

Tenzin narrowed her eyes. "It's not nice when someone messes with your stuff, is it?"

"I didn't damage your damn rapier! The way you had it placed, it almost took out my eye every time I left the downstairs bathroom. So I moved it. I didn't drop it on its hilt from a height of twelve feet!"

"It wouldn't have taken out your eye if you weren't looking at your phone all the time. You should watch where you're going."

"You're making me mental." His hardbacks were still suspended in the air. "Please put my books down. I will tell Giovanni you're abusing them if you don't."

Tenzin had been friends with his uncle hundreds of years before Ben had been born, and they'd worked as assassins for a time. Tenzin wasn't afraid of his uncle, but she found Giovanni's disapproval annoying.

She floated to the ground, still staying in the shadows, and handed him the books. "There. Don't move my stuff again."

"Then don't put it where I could do myself permanent bodily injury, Tiny. Not all of us can regrow body parts if we lose them."

She cocked her head and looked at him. "That is a very slow and painful process, even for vampires."

"And since I'm human, not an option for me. Please don't put your swords in places that will gouge out my eyes."

"Fine." She bent down and picked up a single book. "Here."

He took the book and ignored the dozen on the ground. "Thanks."

Tenzin smiled, all ire forgotten. "You're welcome."

Then Tenzin flew back up to her loft and disappeared.

Ben looked at all the books on the floor. "Do you have any more up there?"

"Yes. Do you want me to—"

"*Don't* toss them down." He took a deep breath. "Hand them down please. After I put these away." He picked up two more books. "Any calls or emails while I was out?"

"No calls."

"But did you check your email?"

"No." She sighed. "I wish you'd never made me an email account. It's not the same as letters."

"I know that, Tenzin, but it's how the modern world communicates. And if you don't check it every day, your inbox will take over the world."

"Is that why you take your phone to the toilet?"

"Yes," he said. "Now check your messages."

Tenzin called, "Cara, check my email."

A polite artificial voice filled the living area. "Checking electronic messages for Tenzin." There was a soft hum before Cara said, "You have five new messages."

"Read subject lines."

She complained about it, but Ben was continually amazed by how quick Tenzin was with technology. She'd had limited access to the electronic revolution until an immortal tech company in Ireland came out with the Noct voice recognition program. Vampire touch wreaked havoc on any electronic gadget because of their amnis, the electrical current that ran under their skin and connected them to their elemental ability.

Wind and water vampires had bad reactions to electronics. Earth vampires could handle some gadgets a little better than others. Rare fire vampires like his uncle could short out the computer in a modern car just by sitting in the front seat.

No computers. No mobile phones. No iPods or tablets or new appliances.

But then came Noct.

"Reading subject lines," Cara said. "From Beatrice De Novo, 'I need a recipe, don't ignore me.'"

"Delete," Tenzin said.

"You should at least write her back," Ben said. Beatrice was his aunt and one of the few vampires who was more comfortable with e-mail than parchment.

"I don't cook from recipes," Tenzin said, "so that would be useless. Next message."

Cara read, "From Blumenthal Blades. 'Desirable saber for your Eastern European collection.'"

"Save," Tenzin said. "That sounds promising."

Ben shelved three more books. "Because you definitely need more swords."

"I always need more swords."

"From Viva Industries," Cara read. "'All natural male enhancement from Asia.'"

Tenzin laughed. "That's what he said."

It took Ben a second to realize Tenzin had actually made a joke, then he grimaced. "Delete!"

"I do not recognize voice signature for the current account," Cara said. "Shall I log out Tenzin?"

"No," Tenzin said. "Delete 'All Natural Male Enhancement,' Cara. Next message."

"From Jonathan Rothwell. 'Confirming details for upcoming travel.'"

"Save," Tenzin said quickly, glancing at Ben. "I'll read that later."

He kept his eyes on his bookshelves. "You going to Shanghai?"

"I haven't decided yet."

Ben tried not to react. Jonathan Rothwell was the personal secretary for Cheng, an honest-to-goodness vampire pirate who ruled Shanghai. He was also Tenzin's ex... something. Former lover? *Current* lover?

It's none of your business. Ben said, "We don't have anything on the schedule, so whatever you want to do."

Ben decided to reorganize the art section of his bookshelves. He'd had the hardbacks arranged by color, but Tenzin had screwed it all up. He might as well reorganize according to style and period.

Tenzin called, "Cara, next message."

"From Novia O'Brien. Copied to Ben Vecchio. 'Monthly meeting at Bat and Barrel?'"

Ben looked up. "Better read the whole thing. She's been

trying to pay off that favor for six months. She and Cormac are getting annoyed."

"I don't care," Tenzin said. "It was a pair of opera glasses, but it wasn't an easy retrieval. I'm not willing to waste a favor so they can mark it off their ledger. Let them be annoyed. Cara, read message."

Cara read, "Good evening. Would love to meet and touch base with the two of you when you have a free night. Gavin's new pub is getting good buzz. Saturday night at eleven work for you two?'"

Ben waited for Tenzin to look at him. "We need to throw them a bone."

"I don't understand the idiom," Tenzin said. She turned her eyes and stared at the opposite wall, swinging one leg back and forth on the edge of her room.

"Yes, you do," Ben said. "Don't play dumb. Throw them a bone. Let them pay us back."

She shrugged. "I don't need anything from them right now."

"It was two days work at the most—"

"And I refused to let them pay us for that reason," she said.

"The O'Briens are a huge clan," Ben said. "They're independent, and they don't like owing people."

She smiled. "Well, they owe us now."

"I know you live for racking up favors," Ben said, "but we live here at their pleasure."

Tenzin laughed.

The vampires in charge of the great city of New York were the O'Briens, a clan of earth vampires who'd taken over the city in a violent coupe and held it through numbers, wise bribery, and clever manipulation.

Ben and Tenzin had moved to New York with the

understanding that Tenzin—an immensely powerful vampire—would demonstrate no ambition that would challenge the current vampires in charge. She would also use her influence and connections in Asia to increase foreign trade.

"All I'm saying," Ben said, "is that unless you want cause an intercity incident, piss off a powerful earth vampire clan, kill a bunch of people, and take control of the city—which obviously you could do if you *really* wanted to —we should probably just meet with Novia and let her do something nice for us so her sire feels better."

Tenzin dropped from her room and hung upside down, her face level with Ben's. Talking to her like that was always disorienting.

That was, of course, why she did it.

"Is there something you need?" Ben asked.

"I'm hungry."

"Doubtful." He'd seen her drink a tall glass of blood three days ago while she was binge-watching a British reality show. At Tenzin's age, she didn't need much blood to survive.

Nevertheless, she glanced down at his neck and licked her lower lip.

"Don't piss me off, Tenzin." That was *not* their agreement. They were partners. He wasn't food.

"Novia said she wants to meet at Gavin's?"

"Gavin always pays the extra tribute to have neutral pubs in every city," Ben said quietly. "She's leveling the playing field, making the effort to accommodate your status. We should meet her."

Tenzin narrowed her eyes. "You meet her first. Tonight."

"Fine." Massaging egos was all part of the vampire package.

Tenzin flew back to her room and Ben continued organizing his books, mentally composing the email he'd send to Novia.

Ben Vecchio may have been born in the Bowery to good-for-nothing human parents, but he'd been raised and mentored from the age of twelve by his adoptive uncle, a fire vampire of fierce reputation and a deep desire to be left alone. Ben knew more about immortal politics than most vampires. Their world operated on a carefully balanced network of allegiances, loyalties, family ties, and favors. It was feudal, but it worked.

Most of the time.

Tenzin watched him as he slept that afternoon.

Shining boy.

The lines around Ben's mouth and eyes had deepened. Not much. But he'd grown from the young man she had known and into the man he would become.

Even so, he was her shining boy, eager to fix problems, fight battles, and seek treasure. He'd dragged her to this metal city and made her a nest in the sky, quick to reassure her of his plans.

It will be brilliant. It will be fun. We'll get rich. Well, I'll get rich and you'll get richer.

Tenzin smiled.

Ben would go to the meeting with the young vampire and charm her into a solution both Tenzin and the New York hierarchy could live with. He'd negotiate with smiles and debate with quips. Ben was both her partner and her better half. He was one of the few humans who'd ever understood her, and possibly the only one who'd never feared her. Even her own sire feared her.

Not Ben.

He picked and poked at her as a hobby. He antagonized her and did it with a smile. She pushed him just far enough to drive him crazy. Why?

It was fun.

Their partnership was good. He was finding his way and meeting his people. Making connections and learning the ways of their world. He had time as long as she was with him. As long as she watched. His human experience would only add to the being he would become.

Of course, he did have that white knight tendency.

She'd have to fix that.

White knights had a tendency to get their armor bloody, and *that* could not happen.

Not until it was time.

For more information about MIDNIGHT LABYRINTH and other upcoming releases, please subscribe to my newsletter at ElizabethHunterWrites.com.

ACKNOWLEDGMENTS

This was a strange book for me, because it was the first book I've worked on in a long time without my friend and developmental editor, Lora Gasway. Is it strange to mention that? I can't stop thinking about it as I think about the planning and writing of this book. We lost Lora late last year, and it was a blow to all of her family and friends.

For those of us who worked with Lora, it also presented the challenge of bridging the huge gap the loss of her expertise and professionalism left behind.

Knowing this, I'm sure you can appreciate the tremendous gratitude I feel for two beta readers who stepped in on very short notice to help me edit this book before it went to my copyeditor, Anne. RJ Blain and Heather Kinne both offered invaluable feedback on very short notice, and did so with grace and compassion. I cannot thank them enough.

I also want to thank my tremendous copy editor, Anne Victory, and my proofreader, Linda. Your insights are invaluable. Your friendship is precious.

Love and appreciation to the lovely and welcoming readers I met both in London and Edinburgh during my research trip for this book. In particular, my guides to Edinburgh, Lara and Stuart Massie, the incomparable Kenneth Hanley, and my hair guru and fellow free spirit Kirsty Williams. You all made my first visit to Edinburgh memorable, warm, and informative. I cannot thank you enough, and I can't wait to return the favor if you ever visit California.

Thanks, as always, to Damonza for their cover work on this book and for understanding that there may be fifty shades of grey, but there are probably *one hundred* fifty shades of green. And this author had to have exactly the right one.

Many thanks to my assistants Gen and Jenn. Both keep me organized and looking my best, both online and off.

Many, many thanks to my family and loved ones who have to put up with my whining about titles for hours on end. And to David, who is patience personified.

And thanks to my amazing reader group on Facebook and the many writing friends who have been so supporting during this tumultuous past year.

Horrible things happened. Amazing things happened.

Whatever comes next, I know I have good people by my side.

ABOUT THE AUTHOR

ELIZABETH HUNTER is a contemporary fantasy, paranormal romance, and paranormal mystery writer. She is a graduate of the University of Houston Honors College and a former English teacher. She once substitute taught a kindergarten class but decided that middle school was far less frightening. Thankfully, people now pay her to write books and eighth graders everywhere rejoice.

She currently lives in Central California with her son, two dogs, many plants, and a sadly empty fish tank. She is the author of the Elemental Mysteries and Elemental World series, the Cambio Springs series, the Irin Chronicles, and other works of fiction.

ElizabethHunterWrites.com
Elizabeth@ElizabethHunterWrites.com

ALSO BY ELIZABETH HUNTER

The Elemental Legacy

Shadows and Gold

Imitation and Alchemy

Omens and Artifacts

Midnight Labyrinth (November 2017)

The Elemental Mysteries

A Hidden Fire

This Same Earth

The Force of Wind

A Fall of Water

All the Stars Look Down (short story)

The Elemental World

Building From Ashes

Waterlocked

Blood and Sand

The Bronze Blade

The Scarlet Deep

Beneath a Waning Moon

A Stone-Kissed Sea

Made in the USA
Middletown, DE
21 July 2018